I0617714

Acquired Desires

Sexy Stories Collection

VOLUME 36

6 EROTIC SHORT STORIES

KELLEN PRIME

Acquired Desires/ Kellen Prime. -- 1st ed.
Xplicit Press, an imprint of TLM Media LLC

ISBN-13: 978-1-62327-567-9
ISBN-10: 1-62327-567-9
eISBN: 978-1-62327-617-1

Printed in the United States of America

.

CONTENTS

1 TABITHA'S TRUTH

It was impossible for Tabitha to learn everything that she needed to learn about being a woman from her father. In fact, there was nothing that he had endeavored to teach her that would prepare her for her role as concubine in the palace. Neither of them had even considered this as an option for the young girl who'd mostly been raised as if she was Clement's son, and not his only surviving child from his true love, Rachel, who had herself been taken in her prime by a bear while out gathering. So Clement and Tabitha had been each other's company since the child was two and had spent sixteen years in the woods hunting, talking, and awkwardly working through the changes in Tabitha that reminded Clement that in fact he had a daughter.Once the raids started, word spread quickly through the woods. Marauding bands had started terrorizing the small kingdom, stealing away virgins for their coming of age sons. It was a fate worse than death, to be violated by a man, or many men from a tribe who didn't share your beliefs, and your spirituality. And to be taken in that way by a man you did not love, and who did not love you, it was simply too much for many families to bear.

The people of the land started to send their daughters away to live with distant relatives far away. Others married sooner than they had planned so that the number of virgins decreased. Pretty soon, the value of a single virgin was so high that rewards were offered outright to anyone who would present a virgin to the renegades. Some did, which prompted an unprecedented act by the king in an attempt to save not only his kingdom, but his people. They were being turned by money and he needed to do something to preserve the virtue of his subjects before it was too late.

This is how hundreds of virgins found themselves in the palace, married to the king or to one of his sons. This is how Tabitha was spared. When the call was made, many desperate families, especially single fathers like Clement, rushed their daughters to the palace, where they would have both husband and protection. But nothing could really have prepared them for life as a wife. They were even less prepared for life as the wife of a man who had many other wives. This was a situation that meant that yours was a life of being on-call for the satisfaction of your husband's bed. There would be no more to the relationship. How could there be?

Even with this in mind though, Clement prepared his daughter as best he could so that she would stand a greater chance of being accepted into the royal harem. The king was open to marrying the virgins of the land, as too were his sons. But naturally like any other man, they would not be marrying people they didn't at least find a bit attractive. So for the first time in her life Tabitha was forced to focus on the feminine side of herself. Her hair became a priority, the long black mane brushed religiously until it shone. Her skin was bathed in milk for long periods and often, fresh blossoms were crushed and included in her warm baths. The final touch was a brand new dress in lavender and white to make her virginity all the more alluring. It was not all in vain and Tabitha found herself married to none other than the king himself.

After weeks in the palace, the day had come for an audience with the king. Seth was a virile man of forty. He was a soldier, a warrior. Standing at seven feet, he was a good height, as were his sons and in fact many men in the kingdom. They were gentle giants though, but formidable warriors. So there really was no safer place for the kingdom's virginity. He would be picking from the last group to have entered his palace and become his wives, a group of virgins from the far end of the woods. Tabitha was in this group of thirty. By the end of the month, none of them would be virgins anymore.

They stand in front of Seth, few of them older than eighteen and the rest of them just. Their hair is braided up so that their faces are clearly seen. They have the softest silk hanging from their bodies such that Seth has easy access to parts of them he wishes his hands to explore. The garments can also be discarded with the pull of a single chord. He makes his way up the row of girls, pulling this chord as he goes. It isn't long before thirty naked virgins stand before him. His face registers pleasure.

Tabitha's discomfort is obvious as she tries to cross her legs standing. Some of the other girls try the same, in vain. They get a reprimanding look from the other older women in the room, the women who prepared them for the king. They reluctantly try to relax. Seth makes his way back down the row, parting legs, kissing some lips, placing a finger menacingly near exposed cunts. There is no room for embarrassment as their husband makes his examinations. They all know that one of them will be deflowered tonight. Hopefully whoever she is will be able to help the rest of them with useful information for when it is their turn.

She can't help shaking when the king nears her. He's no more than two girls away from Tabitha now and since there are less than five girls on the other side of her, her chances are looking slim. It might be her if nobody impresses him. But nobody does and soon, too soon, the king is standing in front of a naked quivering Tabitha. She hates that she's more afraid now of this man than she's ever been of any of the beasts in the woods that she's had to fight off while out hunting with her father. If she had a bow, or even a dagger, she might just kill Seth, instinctively, perceiving him as a threat.

But she can do nothing as he cups her breasts and gives a firm squeeze to the youthful mounds. She can't push him away as he tastes her nipples with his tongue and then sucks on the entire breast, his mouth hot, his beard hard against her delicate olive skin. She wants to turn and run as his hands start to trace down her body, finding her ass and then pulling her toward him as he simultaneously smells her neck and then licks it just before he sticks his tongue in her ear.

The outline of his dick traces well passed her cunt and up her stomach. Seth has a massive cock. His hand finds her cunt and plays with the curls he finds there. His fingers search briefly and then stop when they come upon her untouched clit. A little coaxing and the clit blooms, much to Tabitha's surprise. The king is both pleased and amused. He smiles at her as he wets the tip of his finger and then finds the entrance to her cunt. Her face registers panic as she anticipates the finger inside her. She wants to move away but the king has a hand on her behind that prevents her from moving very far. The others try hard not to watch but pretty soon all eyes are on Tabitha, everyone relieved that she seems to have caught the king's attention.

Seth tries for a little of his finger but Tabitha's cunt is not very accommodating. He looks her in her eyes as he wets the finger again, and again he tries for some entry; again nothing, barely getting half a fingernail in. He finds her clit and draws tiny circles on it, drawing soft moans from the virgin he's deliberately trying to arouse. The circles stay small but the pressure is progressive. Soon Seth is pushing hard on Tabitha's clit, almost as though he expects her pussy opening to miraculously shift to where his finger is and he might get his thick finger inside her. She stumbles, but is held up by the king.

Tabitha can't help the sounds escaping her now as the king's finger works intently on her clit. Everyone seems to have disappeared now, and even the girls on either side of her who hold her up so that the king can concentrate are nothing more than inanimate support pillars to Tabitha, who for the first time in her life is having her pussy touched by a man in ways that she herself had done but a few times in her quiet moments alone when her father had taken the two-day trek to the market. She could only hope that this is what sex would be like. But she knew from the tales shared among the girls that there was a little more to it than a thick finger on the fringes of your cunt.

The smell of Tabitha's moistening cunt hits Seth like fresh blossoms from a spring meadow. He runs his finger up and down a few more times before finding her hole again. This time he doesn't wet his own finger but gently eases it into the hole, just a little. Then he repeats his circles, slowly, very slowly so as not to traumatize Tabitha or bring her too abruptly from the climatic paradise he's managed to get her to. He patiently circles the entrance of her cunt for a few more strokes until eventually Tabitha's pussy gives up its nectar. The inside of her cunt is now wet and she is as ready as she'll ever be for her virginity to be unequivocally lost to his majesty's already throbbing cock.

Seth has made his choice....

Everyone leaves the room, Seth and Tabitha alone now. The king places her on the bed, a large platform of rich silks and cottons, and the feathers of many exotic birds. The linens emit a fragrance familiar to Tabitha from her adventures in the forest. But some of the fragrances are new. They excite and relax her. She watches as Seth pours a golden chalice full of wine. He takes a large sip and then brings the drink to her. She refuses it but he insists, telling her that it will make the night easier. Immediately, her nerves return and she searches for refuge in the bittersweet drink.

The room is lit only by the roaring fire coming from the large fireplace in the wall. Seth removes his robe and stands near the heat, casting a giant shadow against the wall. His penis is still completely erect and Tabitha, who catches it on the wall, immediately needs a larger sip of wine.

Her mind will not allow her to believe that it isn't as big as it seems on the wall. The facts of the matter are clouded by her nerves. She moves away from him as he approaches the bed, trying hard to avoid making eye contact with his dick. Seth climbs on to the bed and immediately pulls her underneath him, locking her between his thighs.

His dick lies across the slit of her cunt and the head of his large member reaches a few inches above her navel. It's not just that his cock is big, but Tabitha, unlike the giant Seth, is rather short. She now realizes that her first time might turn out to be as excruciating as the other girls made it out to be. Still she lets herself be consoled by the fact that this was still better than the alternative. If it was going to be a traumatic experience, then at least she would be traumatized by her own king, and she would do her best to please him in the process.

A few gentle rubs of the shaft against her pussy and soon her clit remembers the sensations of earlier. She dares not make any suggestive moves for fear of letting Seth think she is readier than she actually is for the inevitable. She reclines coyly against the sheets and decides to let the master do what he knows. She trusts that while she is yet to understand the capabilities of her body, the man on top of her had been with enough women to know exactly what to do with her. His approach definitely inspired confidence. There was an absolute control that exuded from him despite his dick seeming to grow more and more impatient.

Seth kisses Tabitha as gently and as passionately as though she was the only woman he had ever loved. He touches her as though she is the only woman in the world. For all intents and purposes, for the night, she is. His finger again finds her clit as he plants kiss after kiss on her full lips. He lets his tongue stray into her mouth occasionally, letting it linger for a while and then taking it back. His fingers dance over her vagina and then massage her clitoris with the same tender passion as his lips display on hers. She starts to surrender to him and closes her eyes.

Her neck finds that his lips are as generous there as they are to her mouth. He kisses her across the entire surface of her neck, lifting her with his other hand so that he can get as far back as possible. She finds the back of her neck to be particularly sensitive and a few giggles escape her. She's embarrassed, but Seth continues kissing her without skipping a beat and so she soon accepts that she needn't be. The pressure on her clit again intensifies, just as Seth settles the fullness of his mouth over her firm breasts. He takes his time enjoying each of her delicious mounds in turn.

Seth moves some ways down the bed so that he can comfortably access her stomach and sides. He kisses and licks her all over her mid-section so that the giggles again make her feel awkward. She had never been touched this way and the newness of it all was juxtaposed with the completeness of her deflowering that loomed in the air. There was no trial run or preparation. This was the preparation. Seth was preparing her to receive his cock in a few minutes. And while he seemed patient now, Tabitha was all too aware of the stories of what happens to a man once he introduces his cock to the warmth of a cunt. The prospect of virgin cunt had driven many men to madness.

The hand on her pussy is suddenly on her thigh and her leg is moved to the side. Her cunt is now open to him and his mouth finds the spot on her clit where his fingers just played. To her absolute surprise, he rests his mouth on her clit and kisses the lips below as he had done the lips above. She is suddenly incredibly aware of herself, her scent, her stickiness. She wants to move away from him and apologize but before she can, his tongue is on her clit and around the entrance to her cunt lapping up all her insecurities. Her smell and her taste are now on his tongue and he seems to be enjoying the shit out of both. Again, she assumes that all must then be well and she gives in to this overwhelming sensation.

Seth massages her thighs, both now in either hand as he pushes her legs apart. He does this gently as he nibbles, as gently, on her cunt lips. His tongue slides around her pussy and slips ever so slightly into it, then out again. He tries to go in a little more but pulls out every time her cunt tenses and strangles his tongue. He resumes the gently licking of her clit that seems to relax her enough for him to make brief entries into the vagina his preparing to completely invade shortly.

Tabitha starts to produce the nectar that was the final deciding factor for Seth earlier. The king's response is more intense than it was the first time and he almost swallows her cunt as he indulges in the juices. She too finds that the fluid escaping her elevates her own arousal, making her feel a little more open to the cock that has its sights set on her. Seth though suddenly seems less insistent on moving his mouth away from her juicy pussy, enjoying the raw responses he's getting from the virgin whose vagina he has in the grips of lips, teeth, and tongue. His tongue now glides in and out of her with little effort as the walls of her cunt are completely coated from the inside.

It seems like hours but it's really just minutes. The thick tongue moves in and out of her cunt, more and more rapidly the more juice she releases. It lingers inside of her occasionally, the king saying things that only her pussy understands. The complete power of Seth's tongue inside of her feels how she had always imagined a cock would feel in her cunt. She had never seen a dick of course before Seth's so while she knew that it was meant to be inside her, she had no idea that men were of the habit of eating pussy with their mouths too. She also had no idea that cocks were this big and suddenly she was curious to know what it would actually feel like inside her. But still she would not be the one to initiate this move.

Wave after wave of pleasure starts to take over her, as she is continually tongue-fucked by Seth. His hands have moved down off her thighs now and his fingers pull her pussy apart so that his tongue can dig deeper and deeper inside of her. She loses control of her waist, as she seems to push her pussy deeper into Seth's mouth. She also grabs his head and pulls him down into her. She wants him in places nobody's ever been. She needs him inside her even though she has no real idea of what that actually means.

Seth does nothing that indicates that there will be anything but his mouth on her pussy and he licks the cunt until Tabitha can no longer hold herself back from spraying her femininity all over the inside of the king's mouth. Seth sucks it up and swallows the excess, lapping the juices up from her thighs as well. Tabitha has just had her first orgasm as a married woman, and the look on the king's face says that she's done so too soon. She apologizes, the king already covering himself with a robe. He takes a sip from the chalice and then tells her to get dressed, that that will be all for the night. She's disappointed him. She knows this. This is confirmed as she passes another woman making her way to the king's chamber as she makes her way from it.

Back with the other girls, she is unable to answer the many questions thrown at her. Eventually, the others let her sleep and she hides her shame in her sheets. She cries with no tears and has no dreams until morning. There is a deep fear inside of her that she might be sent back. What if the king is unsure of her virginity? Was her body's natural response to what he had done to her somehow wrong? She really didn't know. All she knew was that last night she was supposed to lose her virginity but she didn't. She had an orgasm in the king's mouth and then he sent her away. And now, before she's even eaten breakfast, the older women have asked her to their chambers for a conversation.

The room is quiet as Tabitha enters. She isn't greeted, simply acknowledged with a few nods, and then she is immediately undressed by the only two young women in the room. She stands naked before eight women, elders of the harem, and the formal keepers of the younger wives of the kingdom. These women are the custodians of the royal pussy and it is their job to make sure that the women charged with the king's pleasure are able to do just that, please Seth. They are more than qualified to do this having at one time been the younger wives themselves. Tabitha is bathed by the two young women who had undressed her.

It is an unusual feeling for Tabitha to have her body touched by these women, barely older than she is. They take their time about running the scented water, warm and sensuous, all over her perfect body. The marble tub is large enough for all three women to fit in it. They all stand in the knee-deep spring water, fused with a mixture of herbs, petals, and milk, Tabitha in the middle of the two virgins working their hands up and down the full length of her. There are moments when she thinks they might touch her cunt and then their hands glide by. Her breasts and her ass are not exempt from their slippery fingers though.

She is helped out of the bath and has her body examined after the two assistants have dried her completely. They busy themselves braiding her hair while two of the older women start with a mixture that smells of honey and almonds, working it into every inch of her skin. She starts to smell rather edible, even her hair getting generous helpings of berry scents that make Tabitha feel like she were a rather elaborate dessert. She touches herself in anticipation of a sticky sensation. Thankfully, there is none. The mixtures absorb into her skin as easily as they do into her hair, which is now exquisitely braided up half of her scalp, falling in excessive raven tresses down the back.

Still naked, Tabitha is laid on the divan, dressed similar to the king's bed, the same forest fragrances infused into the linens. Nobody has spoken to her yet, but they've spent the entire time talking about her and of the king's desire to have her completely, which would require the preparation being rendered her now by the hands of experience. If Seth was to thoroughly enjoy her, her cunt was going to have to be tamed. And this would have to be done without her losing her virginity, a privilege that was reserved for the king who had saved her. So this entire exercise, this entire day, was dedicated to schooling Tabitha's virgin cunt in the art of pleasing the king.

Her cunt is fondled gently as she lies on her back with her legs parted. Ursula, who happens to be Seth's first wife, the true queen, is the woman with her fingers on the keeper of Tabitha's virginity. Ruby and Laura, the virgin aids, are in charge of keeping her legs apart so that the queen can do her work. Ursula knows her husband. She understands his lovemaking and his needs. She knows better than most how he is most pleased and how to completely satisfy him. She has an intimate understanding of his body and especially his penis. And because she is a woman, an experienced woman, she understands how to deal with virginity.

The queen's fingers on her clit make her uncomfortable. This discomfort is compounded by the fact that still, nobody speaks to her. Tabitha's reflexive movement to close her legs as the external terrain of her pussy is violated against her permission is resisted by the pairs of hands on either leg. Her cunt is the property of the kingdom and so the queen is simply exercising her right over what is essentially hers. In fact, the queen is engaged in one of the most intimate of the ancient practices: that of ensuring that all the younger wives are as capable as she is of caring for the needs of the king. A sexually satisfied ruler is a happy one, she has come to learn.

Ursula indicates to the aids that they should part Tabitha's legs further. They do, and Tabitha closes her eyes and turns her head away from the queen at the same time. With the distance between her thighs widened, she is fondled some more. There is no lubrication or preparation as the queen milks her pussy lips, pulling on them, stretching them. There is no moisture that helps her receive the finger that the queen suddenly introduces into her cunt, making brief entries into her, short stabs barely an inch. There is always the fear that the finger might go too deep and so Tabitha is practically knotted in a ball, thinking she might lose her virginity to the queen. But Ursula and the other senior wives have done this often enough to know exactly what they are doing.

Without warning, Tabitha releases a stream of pussy juice, dressing the queen's finger with it. The other women comment on the haste with which she has climaxed and confirm that they understand the king's concerns. The young virgin has not explored her own body sufficiently to understand its capabilities and so harness its power. She is still left to the mercy of all things external, and as a result she cums quickly. Now this isn't necessarily a bad thing, especially if you are on your own and want to take yourself to that happy place quickly and then get on with the rest of your day. But when the king wants to get maximum pleasure from your cunt, he needs to know that you can go with him for the long haul. Seth has apparently made it clear to the older women that he is attracted to Tabitha and the last thing he wants is to be left fucking her long after she has climaxed, not sure of whether she continues to enjoy his cock inside her after she's had her orgasm. And so it is the duty of the queen and the others to gain an understanding of Tabitha's cunt so that the king knows what to do with it.

After her pussy has been milked four more times, Tabitha is again bathed. This time her vagina is the focus and she has her cunt cleaned so gently she is aroused for the entire duration of the bathing experience. She is clothed in a simple silk cover again and is escorted to the king's chamber. Seth is speaking to Ursula when they arrive. She waits until the queen leaves before she enters the room. The day is not over yet and the sun shines through the high windows in the room. The fire seems to be a constant in the cold stone room and the contrasts of visuals and ambiance are strangely comforting.

Seth too doesn't greet the virgin, removing the silk from her skin and taking long breaths, inhaling her scent. He kisses her body as he moves along it, enjoying the smell and taste of the honey on her skin. The king doesn't need to remove his own silk gown for Tabitha to see that he's already grown a massive erection. But there is not even time for her to focus on Seth's cock as he immediately finds her cunt with his mouth and takes the longest suck from deep inside the fruits of her vagina. He immediately draws drops of cunt dew into his mouth and sucks harder, hoping for more. When the pussy seems to have dried up, he licks the area gently and then lets his tongue check her depths for some more. The walls of her cunt seem to be retaining the fluid that seems to be an effective stiffening agent for his cock. Seth lifts her up and takes her to his bed.

On his back, he places Tabitha over his face and takes her pussy into his mouth. He eats her cunt as she sits on his face. Tabitha has no way of moving off of him as he takes firm hold of her legs and keeps her where she is. She takes hold of her own breasts as the man underneath her shoots his tongue in and out of her cunt. She pulls on her nipples as they enlarge between her fingers. Thumb and index pull the nipples away from the breasts they sit on. She voices her pleasure loudly, pleasing Seth who shoots her with more of his tongue, the walls of her cunt too slippery now to grip the thick meat. She fills Seth's mouth with cum.

He nibbles her clit as he licks her pussy dry. She quivers as he keeps her on him. She lets her hands rest on her hips to steady herself as Seth lifts her just high enough off of her so that he can do a good job of sucking up her pussy's generosity. Each lick brings memories of recent climaxes to the fore. It isn't long before Tabitha is tugging at her mounds, squeezing and pulling on their young firm perfection as Seth quickly takes her back to the beginning of the end. She cannot even brace herself as she falls and rises on his face at his will and fancy.

His consumption of her pussy is more determined this time. Whatever secrets Ursula shared with him about her cunt seem to have his mouth excited and his cock, while stiff, resigned to a patient anticipation. Seth draws from deep inside her the sensations and liquids that he seems to enjoy. She loses her composure again and lets herself go as Seth swallows the inside of her pussy with such force she feels like he's turning her cunt inside out. There are brief moments where she feels his tongue inside of her but the rest of the time she registers nothing but the sensation that the inner walls of her vagina are collapsing from inside her and into the king's mouth.

To Seth's delight, she takes a little bit longer to cum, allowing him to indulge in the pleasures of her pussy a little longer. But when she does erupt, it is in buckets, a waterfall of femininity that Seth laps up with the enthusiasm of a cub on its mother's nipples for the first time. Not a drop is wasted as the king cleans the surface of her cunt while she gathers herself internally. She has stopped anticipating his cock because there seems to be no new interest from the royal scepter toward her peasant pussy. She remains motionless as the king removes his head from under her.

She feels again that she needs to apologize when Seth gets a drink in silence and then stands drinking it by the fire. She covers up and stands near the bed waiting for further instructions. Her apology is met with a slight smile and a dismissive nod. She leaves, not sure anymore what anything means. She knows just that whatever her body seems to be doing isn't what the king would like it to be doing and she has the overwhelming urge to run away and give herself to the renegades. That she has turned out to be a disappointment to the man who gave her the opportunity to be a little more than a virgin plaything to foreign boys is something she can't handle.

Tabitha bumps into another girl as she leaves, a different girl from before but also one that she knows has been with the king before. This beauty must have gotten it right and so she has come to pick up the pieces of her failed attempts with the king. This turns Tabitha's stomach in a cauldron of envy and sadness and she can think of nothing but escape now. She cannot take the shame. Failed by her own womanhood before it has even flowered is something she had not expected. Perhaps if Seth were a lesser man it would have been easier. But this was the king. And she was here because he thought she should be satisfying. All she's done thus far is to quench his insatiable thirst for cunt-juice.

Alone in bed her mind races with thoughts of the king and his cock. When she saw it the first day, she thought it would be in her and done with her that first day. But instead, she got fingers and tongue. Her orgasms were awesome, but they were also quick. The king had not yet had an orgasm in her presence. He had not climaxed with her, or because of her. This was probably why he had had the queen try to treat whatever condition they had decided she had that made her uncockworthy. But it hadn't helped because again Tabitha was replaced with another girl, her scent still on the sheets on which she had had her pussy devoured by the king.

It's too late for her to think too deeply about the details of her troubled cunt but the thoughts that do linger, thoughts of Seth's massive cock, send warm trickles to her cunt. She comforts her vagina by tracing her own fingers over it as thoughts of Seth's rod moving into it warm her even further. She lets her finger enter, just as the king enters her in her imagination. Not too deep so as not to upset the sensation, Tabitha tickles her own cunt while allowing herself to long for the king. She plays with her pussy with a delicate urgency that requires gentle and steady movements in the room where many other women are already lost in sleep.

She lets herself forget that the king won't fuck her as she imagines his long tool reaching inside her and satisfying not just her cunt but also itself. She pictures Seth with his eyes fixed on her as he moves in and out of her. The sound of his breathing, the smell of his skin, the warmth of the fire all come together in her mind, making her believe that inside her is the full length and girth of his majesty's supreme cock. Her own eyes close as she hides in the pillows, muffling the small sounds of pleasure that escape her. Tabitha has forgotten her sense of being slighted now as her own fingers and the vivid images in her head strip her of any sense of inexperience.

She fingers herself with a gentleness that belies the images in her head now as she imagines the king lost inside her, enjoying every inch of her pussy as a warrior enjoys a battle once victory is certain. Seth pushes into her deeper and deeper, her own fingers barely inside her pussy as she deals tender blows to the entrance of her cunt and the clit hanging nearby. She uses both hands as she starts to feel the impending orgasm and hides deeper in the pillow as she pulls harder on her clit. She knows there is no turning back now and suddenly Seth disappears from her mind and it is just her and her fingers in the dark.

She cums, softly, the imaginings of Seth inside her returning as her orgasm reaches its peak and then descends. She brings herself to a complete climax before she dares to look around to see if anyone has heard her. Everyone is still asleep and so she relaxes into the thought that she will have no further embarrassment to deal with. She has had in her mind what she had thought she would have had in reality by now. But the king is not interested in her any longer, at least not like that. So she lets herself accept the worst-case scenario and sleeps having made peace with the fact that she will die a virgin, or be relieved of her position in the harem come morning.

"It's going to be a long day for you today my dear," Ursula is a little more pleasant this morning. Having been summoned by the queen again, she had expected a stern reprimand for not pleasing the king. But instead, everyone greets her with open smiles and light conversation.

"What have I done to offend the king so, that he will not take me?" Tabitha is almost in tears.

"You've not offended him dear, on the contrary. You've excited him, more than he's been in a while. And being the kind of lover that he is, he doesn't want to have an incomplete experience with you. He wants you to derive as much pleasure from him as he is sure he will from you. So we will help you to understand your rather sensitive body, and we will prepare the parts of you that you will use to make his majesty happy." Ursula has said all that needs to be said and Tabitha relaxes.

She allows herself to be bathed again, enjoying the feeling of foreign hands on her this time. She understands the purpose of being bathed now and surrenders to the sensation of fingers not her own. The bath is longer, more drawn out. The hands moving over her don't avoid her pussy now as she is pricked and prodded all over. The scents that float up from the hot water excite her and she too adds her own hands to the ones that finger and feel her. Her thighs are privy to some intense finger action that quickly finds its way to her ass. Her cunt is massaged, every inch of the surface given attention.

Reclining in the bath Tabitha is encouraged by the other women to touch herself. She closes her eyes and lets her hands come onto her vagina, her fingers on her clit. She takes in the warmth around her and palms her pussy over and over again, as she builds up her arousal. She thumbs her clit as the insides of her cunt increase in temperature, her pussy almost as hot as the water she sits in. Her index finger finds her hole and she stirs the entrance to her cunt gently, listening carefully to the guidance she receives. Her thoughts are on the king and his cock the whole time.

She fingers herself gently, her audience watching as she disappears deeper and deeper into whatever the fantasy is that has her eyes closed and her mouth open. She remains conscious of going too deep, taking the focus to her clit every time she thinks she might be getting too excited. Slowly she pulls on her beating clit, thumbing the fleshy flower every time she feels she might climax. She keeps herself from cumming this way a couple more times under the guidance of the women in the room until eventually she is allowed to take herself to orgasm, which she does quickly, disappearing under the water for a moment post-climax.

Her exit from the tub is aided and easy. She is dried and lathered in the honey and almonds from yesterday. Once she is deemed sufficiently edible, she is laid out on the divan again. Tabitha enjoys the attention now, especially since she knows that she has in fact done nothing wrong. Her legs are again parted, as far as they will go this time. The queen approaches her with a 14-inch cylinder that rather closely resembles the king's erect penis. Her composure is quickly lost as she contemplates the possibility that has suddenly presented itself.

The penis in the queen's hand is as regal as the man whose cock after which it was fashioned. Ursula hands it to Tabitha, who feels it between her fingers. Realizing that it has a rubbery texture she is less apprehensive, despite its firmness. The queen had it made by master craftsmen from Persia, as a gift to herself, for the times her husband was away for extended periods. The royal cock is placed in a bowl with hot water and left to sit. It seems to expand under the water. Tabitha has many questions in her eyes but nothing comes out of her mouth, even as she watches the tool being lathered in a clear cream that smells like lavender.

The tip of the tool runs from one end of Tabitha's cunt to the other. The queen's hand is steady as she moves it up and down the line that splits the face of her pussy into east and west. Ursula taps the tool on the pussy, and then rubs it against the clit that flowers as much out of fear as it does out of desire. Then suddenly without warning, the tip of the long penis is inside Tabitha. She gasps, throwing a question mark in every direction.

"Relax Tabitha dear," Ursula reassures her, "we wouldn't dream of robbing Seth of the pleasure of turning you into a woman."

Ursula removes the tool and watches as Tabitha's cunt closes so tightly again as though it was never there. Again, she lets the tool ease into the hole, making it go a little further, a little deeper, and then taking it out. Slowly the sensation of the cock inside of her is no longer traumatic. Slowly it becomes comfortable. Soon it becomes pleasurable. And then, without warning, it becomes the sole focus and desire of Tabitha's virgin hole. Ursula's steady hand continues to feed Tabitha just enough, until eventually, she reaches the wall she knows that only Seth will break, once they have adequately prepared this young woman.

The tool is slowly removed from Tabitha's cunt, and her legs are brought back together and then lifted up, her feet brought almost to her face. She is not prepared for the sensation that follows; the tool suddenly on her never-before-touched asshole. It's too late for her to stop the tool from entering her ass, the lavender cream on it making this effortless. She lets out a rather subdued scream and then gasps as the tool goes nowhere for a moment and then creeps further inside her. "This is a practice the king is fond of, dear, and very few of the others have ever allowed him to indulge in it. It takes a while to get used to but if you can speed up your adjustment, he will be most pleased." Ursula explains what she should have explained before she shoved the representation of her husband's cock up Tabitha's ass. Tabitha continues to gasp as her legs are held in place and the cock is moved in and out of her for as long as it takes her to stop gasping and to start moaning. Ursula feeds her a little too much and again she is gasping, then another scream. The others comfort her, reminding her that hers is to please Seth, who has gone out of his way and exercised great patience because of his own desire to please her.

The tool is removed from her slowly, another, smaller version introduced in its place. Thankfully, this smaller tool also has the same rubber touch, the same warmth, the same I-know-what-I'm-doing-inside-you feel in her ass that the other tool had in her pussy. She immediately enjoys the presence of the smaller cock inside her. Her ass dances around it as the sensation of it moving around inside her registers as pleasurable. This tool is moved in and out of her as the other one was, but with less resistance from her it is given more rigorous motions. Her asshole receives it easily every time the queen removes it completely and inserts it again. Tabitha suddenly finds herself craving the larger royal cock inside her. Her eyes search for it, find it, and speak for themselves.

The queen is pleased with the progress, as are the others. The tool is lifted from its hot water bath again, given another coat of lavender, and inserted into Tabitha's ass gently. Its thickness quickly stretches her asshole, the tight space seeming too compact suddenly. The queen takes her time feeding it to her, not letting any progress be lost by withdrawing. Tabitha takes a deep breath, concentrating on relaxing her ass as she does, following the instructions being whispered to her. The tool makes steady progress into her until just a quarter of it remains outside the ass that was itself a virgin less than an hour earlier.

The queen holds the tool in place, summoning another woman over who rubs her hands in the lavender cream and proceeds to rub Tabitha's belly. Riva, this second woman, an exotic vision from Egypt, makes her way down to Tabitha's cunt and bypassing the clit, slips a long slender finger into her pussy. The sensation of this double penetration has Tabitha panting. She wants to yank the tool from the queen and drive it straight through her virginity, which seems to be the most valuable thing in the room. But instead, she grabs hold of the hands of the other women who have come to help steady her as the lessons of the day start to take on real life.

The tool in her ass starts to move. The finger in her vagina gets life and runs circles along the wall of her pussy. Streams of juice flow out of her almost instantly as she begins too late to process the combination of sensations that she is experiencing. Her climax is loud as she gushes rivers of pussy water all over the scene. She exhales as the sensation winds down and the experience draws to a close. Everyone does a good job of keeping Tabitha together despite her precarious positioning. She tries to look as composed as she can with her legs split, spread and pulled over her head, her cunt wet and her ass occupied by a thick length of rubber.

The tool in her ass fucks her again. In and out the tool moves, more and more of it making its way inside her, until just a quarter of it is outside her again. She enjoys the movements in her ass, the finger in her vagina also getting life again. She closes her eyes as the women working her bring her closer and closer to another orgasm. The queen pushes for more and more of the tool to get inside Tabitha, who doesn't make any discomfort caused by the effort obvious. Tabitha simply moves against the hole that is being penetrated.

The dick is suddenly all the way inside her and there is a pause as everyone watches to see how she is going to respond. The Egyptian finger in her cunt also stalls. Tabitha grabs the hand that the finger protrudes from and pushes on it so that the finger makes a full but gentle entry. There is an audible gasp as everyone watches the finger make a slow exit. For a moment, there is the concern that Tabitha might have breached her own wall, but when the finger comes out clean, there is a huge sigh of relief. The Egyptian plays it safe and removes half of the finger, letting the remaining half dance around, making up in vigor for the absent length.

The tool in her ass is pulled out slowly. Then another complete insertion as her ass is stretched again and again with the tool. Knowing that maximum penetration is possible now by the king puts a smile on the faces of the women who have been tasked with Tabitha's preparation. They try to make her understand that she will be a firm favorite if she can mimic the responses she has had here when she is with the king later.

"Later?" she asks.

"Yes dear, he wants you tonight." Ursula confirms.

So there will be no rest for her even after all the work her cunt and ass have put in today. It probably has to do with taking advantage of the freshness of the stretch, not wanting to risk everything tightening up again over night. The replica of the king's cock is given another hot bath and then inserted into her cunt. It stretches her cunt open uncomfortably, the finger having lulled her into a complacency she couldn't really afford, not now that she will definitely be fucked by the king tonight. The tool is carefully kept in the vicinity of the entrance to her vagina and it is allowed to go no further.

There can be no more risks, Tabitha's cunt practically flowing continuously now with its juices.

She enjoys a long bath alone. This time she is allowed to bath herself. Everyone around her busies themselves with her garments and her cosmetics. Upon exiting the bath, she is massaged long and deep with many oils from exotic lands. Her skin is soft and subtle upon completion. Her hair is not braided this time, just brushed through with olive oil and other nut oils. Her soft curls fall over her shoulders and down her back. She looks like Venus rising fresh from the seashell.

The silk thrown over her is softer than it's been, and scented. This garment clings to her, the fabric seemingly drawn to her skin. She is dotted with fresh fragrances from the recent visit by the merchants and smells like those that nobody has before, many of the perfumes used for the first time. The thin sandals on her soft feet carry her towards the king, who has already sent for her. She is anxious now, knowing that she will definitely not leave his chamber a virgin. It isn't the loss of her virginity that bother her, but rather that this is the only part of the sexual experience that she is not in some way prepared for. She knows that the king's cock will fit inside of her, back and front. But she doesn't know what the sensation will be when it breaks through her internal barrier, and then pushes beyond it.

She waits outside for the king to call her. He seems to take forever despite having already summoned her. There are preparations inside that she cannot see and she tries to imagine what they could be. Nothing in the room seems to need any real changes, and none seem possible given that everything inside the king's chamber seems to be such a fixture. Instead of working herself up about it, Tabitha instead concentrates on her breathing and determines to breathe deep despite any discomfort and to please the king no matter what. Tonight just has to be the night.

Her nerves are finished as she realizes that no matter what she may try to tell herself, tonight will be the night. Too much has gone into the day, into her, for it not to be...

Inside the room, there is nothing changed accept for the addition of fruits and a few other drinks. Tabitha accepts everything that she is offered and even finds the drink warm and soothing. It is the finest wine, sweet and full. Her second drink is as easy to finish as the first, the king pacing himself against her sips. The berries and grapes fed to her are delicious. Some nuts mix with the fruits, adding a nice variety of textures in her mouth. When she refuses any more the king gives her a long look.

He kisses her on her mouth, taking into his mouth whatever traces of fruit and wine linger there. His tongue in her mouth is thick, and hot. He moves it around inside her mouth and locks his tongue with hers. He sucks on it gently, and then releases it, wrapping his lips over her bottom lip. After playing with her bottom lip for a moment her top lip is taken between his. He runs his tongue across her lips briefly before taking them almost completely into his mouth. He's in no hurry and enjoys her mouth for an eternity.

His hands are on every part of her as he kisses her. Seth lets his tongue and his lips travel all over Tabitha as he reveals her to the roaring fire by discarding her silk covering. It drops to the floor as the king drops to his knees and starts to kiss the front of her thighs. He then parts her legs and kisses the inside of her legs. Tabitha has no way of steadying herself and relies on the king to keep her standing upright. Seth's mouth works up her leg and soon he has found her cunt.

Seth shoots his tongue straight into

Tabitha's cunt and keeps it there. He pulls her close and holds her against his face as he loses all gentleness and fucks the pussy with such firm vigor that she quickly moistens as her cunt flows. Seth manages to get Tabitha onto his shoulders with her pussy firm in his mouth. He stands up, raising the woman's pussy seven feet in the air. He holds her in places as he eats out her vagina and she becomes lightheaded for being so high up so suddenly. She is grateful that she can at least grab on to his head for support.

He carries her to the bed on his shoulders and doesn't remove his mouth from her cunt as he lays her down on the bed. Seth continues to enjoy the taste of Tabitha until she feeds him her signature scent, all too quickly. But Seth knows that she is ready to be taken, and so he doesn't let the first flow from her rivers dissuade him. He turns her over and sends his tongue into her ass. She is completely riveted by his continuance and raises her ass so that the king can get into it as deep as he wants. Seth is soon devouring her perky behind.

She doesn't expect the finger that slips into her cunt while the king is still tonguing her ass. But a thick middle finger is inside her pussy, stirring its juices and drawing more and more moisture from the cunt. He gives her no more than an inch of his finger. This is all he needs to feed her, her ass moving in circles in his mouth, her pussy dancing on the finger. He continues to stir as she wets the finger so much that he has soon slipped dangerously deep inside her. He pulls her off his finger and then turns her around so that she faces him.

His balls hang in front of her and she instinctively takes them into her mouth. She licks them, completely coating them, and then takes the large sack into her mouth. She lets the set dance around in her mouth, between her teeth and over her tongue. She sucks on his balls and enjoys them almost as much as she did the strawberries. His balls fill her mouth completely and the warmth of her tongue fills his cock. He is getting closer and closer to fucking her. She can feel it. Looking at his cock, she can see it too.

Seth pushes his fucker towards her and she mouths the tool. He thrusts into her mouth as she raises her ass to the ceiling, facing him on all fours. She sucks his cock as he fucks her mouth. This is something she's never done before but Seth guides her so that she follows easily. He doesn't need to speak his instructions. She senses his desire and loves the feeling of the mammoth dick in her mouth. She also enjoys that she is finally getting an idea of the king in action. His thrusting into her mouth wets her pussy even more, her desire for him to fuck her fast and fuck her hard heightening even more as he starts to drip king-cum into her mouth.

She takes the part of his dick that doesn't fit in her mouth in her hands. Her delicate fingers work up and down the cock as it moves in and out of her mouth. More and more cum falls from the cock and into her mouth and the king is pleased that the taste of him doesn't offend her. She seems to get as much pleasure from the contents of his cock that he does from the product of her pussy. Seth watches his cock in her mouth, his shaft between her fingers. More jizz spills out of the tool at the sight.

Suddenly she is carried away with the sucking. Seth is distracted by the visuals and loses himself in the thrusting. Without warning, Tabitha's mouth is suddenly filled with warm semen. She is confused for a moment but then instinctively swallows as the king continues to thrust into her mouth, unable now to stop himself. He lets his dick rest in the back of her mouth as the last of his load is expelled. She keeps her mouth closed on the cock and manages to swallow the excess. Seth pulls his cock from her and gets her a drink. He takes a large sip before handing her the chalice.

His cock is quickly flaccid. Tabitha's

fears start to resurface. Seth gets onto the bed, on top of her, and starts to insert his flaccid cock into her. She is a little thrown by the sensation, which reminds her suddenly of the replica. He gets four flaccid inches inside of her tight cunt. Tabitha can't believe the strength of the dick, even in its soft state. Seth puts his mouth on Tabitha's. He strains to do so because of his height. She eventually releases his lips and instead takes his nipples into her mouth, an easier move for both of them. Seth appreciates that he can stretch out, despite forgoing his desire to look at her.

He starts to push down on her. He thrusts his flaccid cock, not removing an inch, not adding an inch either. Seth simply moves gently round and around, towards her and then away, creating as much sensation for his soft meat in the tight space. His cock starts to harden as he thrusts. Tabitha immediately has the sense that she is being filled. The growth of the cock speeds up and suddenly the four flaccid inches are four rock-hard inches of the king's cock. And there is nowhere for the dick to go but in. She knows that this is probably it. She tries to remember the sensation from when the queen filled her with the imitation cock. Nothing comes to mind as her cunt suddenly feels overwhelmed and trapped.

Another inch is inside her, then another. She feels the pressure of Seth's humungous cock against the inside of her pussy. This is where the queen had stopped. This was his domain. He was about to do what they had prepared her for. But still, the pressure of his cock against the fragile inner wall of her cunt, the irreparable barrier he is about to break, is almost too much for her. She reminds herself to breathe. She can't. Tabitha can't even think as Seth gives her cunt a few gentle thrusts, slowly pushing back against the wall, slowly weakening it. He gives a few firmer thrusts. Still she is unable to breathe. Eventually she takes a loud deep breath as Seth makes a bold attempt for the wall and breaks through the tiny piece of tissue that had kept him from reaching her depths.

As she exhales, he pushes a little deeper, a little further into her. She is still overwhelmed, not yet fully processing the sensation of being fucked. In spite of its size, Seth's cock is gentle inside her. He fucks her gently, slowly inserting more and more of his cock into her on each stroke. She determines not to hold him back, wanting him to experience the fullness of her. His fucking remains gentle as she slowly starts to build towards her first full orgasm. In and out his scepter moves, inching into her more and more each time, until he finally makes a complete entry. Again, she cannot breathe. And again, she tells herself that she will not make her discomfort known. Unable to see her face he continues to fuck her, and her pussy continues to offer up liquid relief that makes his full penetration more and more pleasurable, elevating it quickly to fucking awesome.

Seth sinks his entire shaft into her a few times before remembering that he needs to let her pussy breathe. He withdraws slowly and lets his cock find her ass as his hands lift her legs. His dick is taken into her ass in one stroke. She manages to breathe this time, a deep inhalation as he drives his cock almost entirely into her on the first attempt. She knows the feeling will improve and so she waits it out with a few silent pants as the king rams her ass, his cock suddenly aware of itself. In and out, he moves his shaft until eventually it is Tabitha pulling him deeper into her. He pounds her ass until he knows it's time to send it home.

His penetration of her pussy is done by a rock-solid python this time. He sends his cock all the way into the back of her vagina and then immediately begins a savage thrusting. All her preparations were for just this, that the king, upon being received by a cunt, became a monster. He fucked like he fought, like a champion assured of victory. Tabitha knew that she was going nowhere now until Seth was satisfied. She didn't mind, his cock inside of her exceeding all her expectations. He surpassed all her fantasies and then some, adding new ones with each swift stroke of his sword.

She doesn't know when she's cum, only that suddenly Seth seems to think that there is more space in her then there is, and that he has more cock than he has, because all of a sudden he is pushing into her so fiercely she feels like he might just send his cock right through her. He fucks her into a delirium; she feels like she's been knocked senseless by powerful opiates. Relentlessly the warrior on top of her fucks her, no signs of relenting. Deep into her he continues to drive his tool, not even pausing when she screams and squirts rivers onto the bed. She has managed to find the source of her vagina's floods and opens the gate. Seth goes crazy, slipping around inside her, falling deeper into her for lack of resistance.

She cums in loads, and still he keeps fucking her. He manages to extract two more orgasms out of her before he starts to feel that he too will shoot shortly. She is caught in one extended climax as Seth rams his tool into her cunt which has started to dry for all the friction. His cock makes full entry with each thrust and lodges itself inside her for moments before making a partial exit. She hears his grunts, and his heavy breathing. He strains against her, inside her. He pushes her into the bed as he himself presses hard into the linens. Finally he shoots, filling her with the hottest feeling inside her, his seed whitewashing her walls. She is a queen who has just felt the full measure of a king. She is a woman who now knows the strength of an able man. He takes a moment before fucking her again, taking longer to cum this time. When he eventually does, he manages to stay with her for one drink and a long kiss. Then he goes to that place most men go after awesome sex.

Tabitha takes a moment to gather herself. She looks over to where the king is asleep. Briefly, the fullness of what has happened overwhelms her. She looks at her pussy, and then over to where the king's limp penis falls from his crotch onto the bed where he lies on his side. There is no doubt that she is now a woman. Whatever questions she had had about that have all been unequivocally answered by the king's dick. She gets off the bed and throws the silk over her head. She takes a sip from the chalice Seth had drunk from and palms a handful of grapes. There is no girl in the passage coming to replace her tonight. There's no need. And Tabitha knows that now that Seth has discovered and introduced her to her truth, that part of her that is woman, she knows that she will be back in the king's bed before too long....

2 CADENCE IN MUMBAI

The heat in Mumbai lives up to every expectation. Cadence isn't sure if she can wait for the hotel shuttle to arrive and starts to look out for another taxi. But even the taxis are flying through. No sooner are they pulling in to the pick-up point, than they are swiftly occupied by other arrivals unable to handle the Indian sun. The 23-year-old journalist from London is in need of air-conditioning, even more than she is in need of the facts that will help her in the match-fixing story she's here to cover.

The hotel isn't altogether unpleasant. It's the standard tourist-on-a-budget outfit that spends the portion of its funds that would otherwise have gone to luxurious fixtures, on the loud box in the wall, which is thankfully keeping the temperature in the room crisp and cool. Despite the relief, Cadence's red hair, usually a conditioned curly mop, is plastered to her head and face. She splashes some more water on her lightly freckled face and turns her hair into a neat bun, keeping whatever damage the heat does between the hotel and the training camp of the team she's going to interview to a minimum.

"This is Cadence from London. She'll be covering our journey for her small paper back in England. Please avail yourselves for her questions and make sure that she gets the best impression of the team." The team's manager, Vimal, speaks both to her and the team. Everyone is pleasant for the most part and Cadence senses none of the usual suspicion with which her and her colleagues are usually greeted.

The journalist makes her way through the team, introducing herself again so that she can get their names. She knows who they are of course, having done her homework. She also knows the members of the team that are involved in the match-fixing scandal, and so she makes an extra effort to be relaxed with them. It is imperative that she wins them over so that they can be comfortable enough around her in order for her to do her real job.

Of course, Vimal is fully aware of why she is here. Yes, his team, the Mumbai

Masters, has had a phenomenal run since their acceptance into the professional league, but then they started to lose some very strategic matches. This raised some suspicion in the betting circles back in London, and Cadence's editor, secretly a betting man himself, put the novice on the story. She had earned her stripes, and this break was a good way of rewarding the tenacious young newshound.

The last person she is introduced to is Rajith Mammen. Rajith is the star wicketkeeper, the team's golden boy with the superb eye and the incredibly uncanny ability to catch. He is also incredibly attractive, dark, and handsome. At 25, he has not only an open face that makes him easy to trust but also the kind of eyes that make you feel like you haven't quite 'met' him, even after an hour of conversation. For this reason, Vimal has appointed Rajith as Cadence's distraction, his assignment simply to keep her from exposing them and disrupting what is proving to be a rather profitable side business.

She can't hide that she immediately finds him attractive, standing closer to him than she needs to. Her eyes search his a little too intently and so she pulls them away, landing on his cock instead. The bulge is almost unnecessary she thinks, but there it is. The soft cloth of his track pants is unsympathetic to the size of his cock. Every move that Rajith makes confirms the generous proportions of his dick for Cadence, who finds herself losing composure quickly, and so she exits after a brief word with Vimal.

As she makes her way out of the door and into the hall, Rajith confirms success by throwing a look at Vimal and then grabbing his cock in his hand, giving the dick a few solid tugs. Vimal is pleased. Rajith himself is not too unhappy. If he is going to be using his cock to distract the naïve little redhead, it does help that she is an attractive piece of ass. The pale pussy wouldn't be his first choice on a regular day, given that he has his share of exotic Indian beauties throwing themselves at him all the time, but once his cock is inside her, chances are that it won't know the difference.

Back in her room, Cadence processes the meeting. Instinct tells her that Rajith had flirted, but she tries to override instinct with common sense. He had no reason to find her attractive. She was the typical 'Lois Lane,' a nerdy little girl with obvious freckles. Her awesome body was thanks to a very sports-oriented private school and yoga, but other than a killer body, nothing about her was interesting. She can't remember exactly what constituted the flirtation, only that the sight of his cock moving under the pants he wore made her uncomfortable. And now, alone in her room, she knows why: she wanted it!

Her virginity was lost early – at sixteen. She was in love, as most girls are, and he was a teenager with a hard cock. But despite having been sexually mature early on in her life and not altogether inactive since, she had never been presented with the opportunity to explore lovemaking beyond the standard British fare she was always offered. Before this trip, she had never been outside of the United Kingdom; within its borders, none of the more exotic Brits seemed to fancy her. So her pale cunt had only ever been fucked by similarly pale penis. That she now has even the slightest possibility of treating her pussy to a spicy alternative excites her enough to have her pull her panties down, part her legs, and feel for her privates in the privacy of her room.

Her pussy soon lets her know that while it's nice to be in the company of familiar fingers, this was a hotel with tourists who would probably be hanging around the bar and pool with thoughts of fucking solidified with every drink consumed. She covers up her cunt and makes her way downstairs in nothing but a bikini and sarong. Having already worked herself up considerably, there was no time to be too fussy over who would be fucking her, and so she makes the deliberate effort to scan the scene for an easy target. It was easy to pick up blokes at the local pubs back home because they were always horny and always pissed. This is a different ball game. At the far end of the pool bar, she finds her mark at last: a spectacled geek with rather long, skinny, legs. She moves in his direction and makes herself visible.

"Can I buy you a drink?" The geek is American.

"Sure!" An American will have to do.

Cadence stands between Landon's legs as she sips on her daiquiri. She notices that the blonde hair on his arms and legs matches the hair on his head and that he too is freckled. His conversation lets her know that he is in fact a super geek of the Internet kind and that he and a few friends were in Mumbai on a summer exchange with a huge Internet firm. It takes two more drinks before Cadence is brave enough to make him aware of the request her pussy has been making in steady beats between her legs since she planted herself between his. She doesn't need to ask Landon twice.

In her room, Landon pulls down his shorts before the door is even closed. Cadence goes to the bed and fumbles in her purse. She hands Landon, already naked, a pack of condoms she's had in her bag for a couple of weeks already. There is no expectation that he will romantically help her with her bikini while kissing her, and so she removes her own covering while he covers his cock. Her bikini hasn't hit the floor when Landon bends her over the bed and sends his long, thick cock straight into her cunt, rolling the remainder of the condom down his cucumber as it disappears into her cunt.

She stumbles forward and looks for something to hold on to, the corner post of the bed the closest thing to her. Landon doesn't need to hold onto any part of her as his cock has filled her pussy and created a rather secure grip from the inside. In an effort to steady herself a little more, Cadence lifts her one leg onto the bed and places her foot firmly on the mattress. Everything is happening too quickly, but she is the one who asked Landon up for an afternoon fuck so she cannot complain. He was now fucking her. His cock pushes against every inch of her pussy as he sends it into her. There is enough of it left outside her vagina for his hand to wrap completely around it. Cadence has a refreshingly tight cunt, and even though his cock is on the super side of large, Landon is of the experience that a bitch who asks for sex is generally possessed of a rather loose pussy.

Her fingers manage to find her clit as

the dick inside her shakes things around a little more. Landon's cock doesn't seem to leave her pussy even though she can feel the drag on her cunt every time he withdraws and the push into her as he thrusts. The presence of cock in her is undeniable. Finally, Landon's hands take firm hold of her ass and move her back and forth over his meat, his thrusts into her done at double time just to mix things up. Her clit is grateful for the preview of the show playing out inside her cunt.

The complete withdrawal from her cunt leaves her momentarily confused, her climax put on pause. She hears Landon fumble another condom. Had he cummed? She doesn't think so. Nothing about the last few thrusts indicated as much. There is suddenly a finger in her ass. It moves around a few times and then is gone. Then a cock – thick and hard – was inserted into her in a swift deliberate movement. She lets her fingers find her cunt when it becomes obvious that his cock is going all the way. She sinks her fingers as deep into her vagina as the position allows while Landon thrusts in and out of her ass, which warms up his dick rather quickly. His dick doesn't leave her ass as her fingers lead her cunt to climax in the air-conditioned room.

Landon extracts his cock and Cadence falls onto the bed. He turns her onto her back and she watches as the third condom in the strip is removed from its packaging and is rolled down to what she can, for the first time, see is at least ten inches of veiny circumcised cock. He doesn't give her too much time to get her bearings on his cock, and he leans over her, sending his cock into her wet pussy. Most of his cock manages to find the inside of her cunt for all the wetness and he fucks her hard. She grabs the bedding and pulls up on the linen, taking fists full of fabric between her fingers as she concedes to the massive rod inside her. He fucks her hard for a solid hour.

The inner walls of her vagina release more liquid. He shoots his cock deeper and deeper into her as the condom is coated in her slippery goo. She cums again and again as his thrusts remain uniform. He drills into her with all the determination of a miner extracting the earth's wealth from its depths. She releases three loads thanks to the cock inside her, and she watches for any indication that Landon might shoot his own load, but nothing. Instead, he checks to see that she has the signature look of satisfaction he and his cock are famous for. She has it along with a smile and an almost embarrassed inability to look him in his face. He enjoys this part.

Her cunt is too wet for him to bring

himself to climax so he pulls out his cock and removes the condom. She watches him work on the meat with his hands, taking turns with left and right as his cock starts its steady climb towards climax. She gets on her knees and swallows his nuts as he gets closer and closer to shooting. She checks that her mouth on his balls isn't a distraction, and when he pulls her back towards his sack, she sucks harder and more intently, going with his flow. There is no warning as suddenly warm drops of cum rain down onto her face. She lets him shoot his load onto her face without wiping it away; giving him the final visuals he had in mind when he started to shoot.

In the shower, she still can't get Rajith out of her mind despite Landon's cock having signed her cunt's death warrant for the night. She washes the day's heat off of her and also the afternoon's tryst. She knows that there will be no more Landon for the remainder of her stay. It was a total once off, the initial 'shall we fuck' approach sealing this. So Landon fucked her so that he wouldn't be forgotten and also so that he would be able to make it a day or two before another cunt made its way to him. She has forgotten him in her head already though despite her pussy having vivid memories of the American pole that brought it to its first multiple orgasms this year.

The conditioner in her hair smells like cinnamon, and Cadence lets it sit while she stands in the breeze, her window open for the first time as the night brings a natural coolness that makes the air conditioner unnecessary. She reminds herself why she's here and takes in the vibe of Mumbai as it filters up from the streets to her room. The city looks different at night. The dark hides the lack of solid infrastructure and also the madness. It looks almost inviting under the cover of darkness, and thoughts of wandering the streets of the city at night start to appeal to Cadence, who feels suddenly like a tourist and not a journalist.

The notes from the meeting earlier again offer her nothing more than memories of Rajith and his cock, and so she decides to make deliberate efforts to formulate a strategy that will keep her away from him. After all, the manager, as well as two or three other players including the captain, was her mark. The wicketkeeper was just that: a skilled catcher. So there was really no reason for her to be too involved with Rajith. The strategy starts to develop in her head and on the paper in front of her as the streets below take on a real life and the sounds become more and more inviting.

Cadence decides to go out for some late night digging so that she can see just how much of the information she has is actually correct. The streets are busy, but in the cool night air, they morph from the day's unbearable to exciting. The digital camera in her hand makes her look more and more like a tourist, and under this guise, she tries to get a general feel of what the public opinion is on the matches lost by the Mumbai cricket outfit that rose so dramatically – and swiftly to cricket greatness. Her cunt also appreciates the walk after the hectic afternoon workout. The breeze between her legs soothes her pussy enough for it to start losing its memory of the recent cock it swallowed.

The sun streams through the light curtains and wakes Cadence. She makes it to the bathroom twice before noticing the note that was probably slipped under her door while she slept – or even while she peed or brushed her teeth. She reads the few words scribbled on the paper that comes from one of the pads the hotel she's in supplies to each room, and there is a brief moment of panic as she thinks the paper may have come from the pad in her room. She looks over to the pad on the side of the bed and then back at the note, but then decides that the information is more important than her panic. She jumps into the shower and then rushes out, following the instructions she's been given.

It isn't difficult for her to find the alley. Walking down it takes some effort though. She manages to psyche herself up eventually and enter the darkness. The movement of people on the bridge overhead makes her a little more comfortable. If anything should befall her, then there will at least be people close by to come to her aid. The alley is in fact a tunnel that runs under a walkway. The other end is brightly lit from the sun that beats down from somewhere above them, but as she gets closer to the center of the tunnel, it is almost pitch dark. Cadence has the urge to run towards the light ahead or turn back towards the light she's left behind. Suddenly she is grabbed from the back and pushed against the wall.

"Don't look back," a husky whisper, the voice distorted deliberately.

The man behind her speaks into her ear. He speaks slowly and has her to nod her head if she understands what he has said. She nods often. The feeling of cock on her thigh is unexpected, and she imagines he must be wearing traditional dress without underpants to stop his cock from dangling uncontrollably and bumping into her as he moves. He's also moved in closer than he needs to for him to speak in her ear. There is no need for his cock to be pressed up against her ass, unless he wanted it there. Cadence moves back against the dick, wondering if every man in this country possessed so much cock.

"I can hear you just fine without your dick repeating everything you say to my ass," she eventually feels the need to say something when he starts elevating his cock, brushing and thrusting.

Instead of moving away, he pushes her into the wall, grabbing her tight at the hips and then pulling her back against his dick. He pushes his dick against her cheeks and then finds the split in her ass through the skirt she has on. Cadence is suddenly overwhelmed by his smell – a mix of woods and spices. She is aroused by the scent and is suddenly more aware of the size of his dick. She takes a deep breath and returns the focus to the information she was promised. More random bits are fed to her along with a couple of thrusts from a cock that is getting considerably stiff and, as such, considerably large.

"Who are you?" she has to ask.

"That is not important. I will be in touch with more information. Do not try to identify me or else I will not be able to help you." The whispers are now clearly deliberate attempts to obscure identity. He rubs his cock against her some more, and she moistens at the touch. The thrill of this stranger with his cock against her in the dark alley turns her on immensely, more so than she would admit to anyone but herself. Something about the heat has her cunt on high alert.

Cadence wants to turn back, wondering why somebody she doesn't know would have to hide himself from her. But she is a journalist and she understands how sensitive sources can be. She decides that the story is more important than the identity of someone she will never have any dealings with after the story breaks, and so she stares at the wall until she can no longer hear the flip-flop of sandals moving away from her and leaving the tunnel. When all is silent, she turns around slowly and looks in both directions. There is nothing but a woman reprimanding a child whose hands are dripping with ice cream, from what Cadence makes out from the yelling.

She's flustered by the time she gets to the match, the Mumbai Masters playing an ODI. She tries to concentrate on the match but is distracted by thoughts of being fucked by strangers in alleys in Mumbai. She lets herself play the 'what if' game and imagines that the man in the alley lifted her skirt and offered her information in exchange for her cunt. Her legs parted; she feels his fingers feel for her panties, pulling them aside and then impaling her to the wall with his cock as it drove into her. The match comes to a rowdy end, the Mumbai Masters having lost, and so Cadence has to bring herself from the alley, remove the strange cock from her pussy, and make her way to the dressing rooms to have a chat with the team.

Outside the dressing room, she waits to be called, the coach and manager having a chat with the players. Vimal sounds angry, the coach trying to calm him down but also sounding like he has no real idea of what happened on the pitch. They discuss the loss in technical terms, and some of the other players sound as confused as the coach. Vimal tries to make everyone understand that this is the nature of the beast and assures them that they have nothing to worry about. He will speak with the team's owners and let them know that things will improve and the team will get back to their top form.

Cadence listens as the team leaves the room through the emergency exit. She wonders why she hasn't been called yet but lets it go for the moment, thinking that a meeting with Vimal should answer some of the more pressing questions. She can always get to the team later in the evening when everyone is a little more relaxed. She enters the room expecting to find Vimal and the coach. Instead, Rajith is in the dressing room alone, naked. She's entered too soon. Or is it too late? Rajith, instead of turning away from her, turns towards her and watches as her eyes fall on his thick twelve inches.

She can't take her eyes off his cock as he speaks to her, totally oblivious to the awkwardness of the situation. Cadence throws her eyes around, hoping for another presence, hoping for Vimal and the coach, or anyone. But the room is empty except for her, Rajith, and his Indian king cobra. His cock is uncircumcised, and the foreskin hangs well over the end of the massive cock. There seems to be too much of it. But it could also be that Cadence has no prior experience with foreskins, and so any skin over the head of a cock will appear to her to be too much.

"You were looking for Vimal?" Rajith squirts moisturizer on his hands and then rubs it into his skin. He makes sure that every lathering ends with his cock, ensuring that Cadence's eyes are never away from his cock for too long.

"Yes." Cadence can only manage one word.

Vimal watches from between the lockers

as Rajith lures Cadence into his web. He stands back as Rajith speaks with Cadence while rubbing his cock, drawing blood to it, growing it steadily. The massive cock doesn't rise. It just hangs lower, the head making a tentative appearance out of the skin covering it. Cadence is lost to the sight, unable to process questions or answers. She simply stares at the massive tool attached to the incredibly handsome, incredibly hairy cricketer. She is no longer aware of herself.

Rajith gets to her, standing in front of her before she knows what is going on. He pulls her to him, holding her against him but keeping his cock to himself at first. Cadence strains away so as not to make any contact with his cock, having had her fair share for the day and not needing to make herself any hornier than she already is – and has been since she left the tunnel.

"You wouldn't be wrong if you thought I wanted to fuck you," he says when he's pulled her close enough for his cock to touch her thigh where her skirt ends.

"You would be wrong if you think I'd let you!" She has resolve in her words that her actions contradict.

"Maybe once this is over, maybe then?" Rajith is persistent. The arrogance in his voice is attractive.

"Maybe, but for now I just want to be

objective about covering your team. You and your cock might just distort my impression of the Mumbai Masters...." She plays the same game he is playing and watches for his response while taking in his scent – a familiar spicy mix.

"So you'd be open to some fun with me and my cock?" He drags it out a bit.

"I'd probably be a whole lot more open after the fuck by the look of things. But after I'm done with my story, we can talk of fucking." Cadence leaves as Rajith's cock finally starts to make an ascent towards her, defying gravity. She makes a note to call Vimal when she gets back to the hotel and set up some group interviews for later in the afternoon. The picture of Rajith's cock has wet her cunt considerably though and it seems to take forever for her to get into her room.

She opens the door and barely notices the note on the floor. She picks it up but decides to read it later, her mind occupied with a more pressing matter. She kicks off her sandals and pulls down her panties as she stumbles towards the bed. She throws herself onto the bed and then pulls her skirt off and throws it on the floor. She pulls her top off, throwing it too on the floor, needing to be naked. She hasn't even noticed that the air conditioner isn't on.

Cadence lets her fingers go straight into

her moist cunt. Three fingers make a quick entry and then wriggle around inside her so as to activate the inner walls. Her pussy wraps around the fingers as Cadence feeds her imagination with images of Rajith and his member – visions of the tool inside her all the way as the wicketkeeper guides the serpent around her garden. She lets the fingers on her other hand join the pussy plundering, and with her eyes shut tight, Cadence rips her pussy apart and then pushes it back together, and pulls it apart and then reaches her fingers deep inside the slippery tunnel so that it can gather itself as she exits again and repeats the delicious exercise.

The massive load she squirts across the linen forces her to remove the bedclothes. She curls up and lets a few fingers stand guard in the general vicinity of her cunt in case Rajith's cock makes a nocturnal visit. Visions of the dick call on Cadence a couple of times, and by the time the sun sets, she has neither the energy nor the desire to make any trips or phone calls. She brings herself to a steady final orgasm in the shower and then falls asleep on the divan by the window, which she has opened now with the room closely resembling the inside of an oven, or Cadence's super-heated cunt.

There is no apprehension this time as she walks into the tunnel. When the stranger steps out of the darkness and pushes her against the wall, she isn't surprised, anticipating cock and so offering no resistance. She makes the conscious effort not to push her ass out in search of the dick that got her wet the last time she was here. There's nothing but hot whispers in her ear for a while though.

Finally, she feels it, the dick, low on her thigh just below her ass. That one person possessing so much cock seems unreal. But Cadence has enough physical evidence to confirm its existence. The mammoth dick moves against her as its owner feeds information into her ear. Again there is nothing told to her that she doesn't already know, and so the most exciting thing about the meeting is again the cock she now wishes would just find her cunt already.

Her pussy is wet. She knows this despite the sweat running down most of her. The inside of her cunt craves the cock that hangs inches behind her, taunting her by touching against her and then moving away. Her story now seems a distant dream as the current reality takes complete hold. Up and down the cock moves against her, its head still pointing to the ground because Cadence is sure what she feels is the top surface of the shaft, the head touching her occasionally from its low vantage. It's the kind of cock that she is sure could do a serious job of fucking her whether or not it was hard.

More information is offered up as her ass is parted and the cock is placed in her sweaty valley. It isn't by accident that Cadence has no underwear on, and with her skirt lifted above her ass and the cock on her naked flesh, the possibility suddenly frightens her. The hot flesh on her flesh brings her to an anticipated reality she suddenly wishes was a dream. If only this were happening back in her room. But here, in this public place, her body would never relax enough to receive this dick that has made her completely incapable of understanding a single word that is being spoken to her.

The entire situation starts to fade more and more into an obscure illusion, the only thing real being the feel of the man's cock on her ass. And his smell, a familiar scent that registers in the back of her head but not completely. There is recognition every time she inhales the wood and spice that seem to permeate from the stranger as he speaks, as he sweats. How could she know this man? Of course, she is remembering his smell from the last time but still. There's more.... Cadence is sure that it is impossible, but still she tries for a link between her recognition and her memories. She takes deep breaths, willing herself to make some sort of association with the fragrance and someone familiar.

It hits her and she pushes back on the cock before turning around. Her mouth is ready, the name of the man she thinks he is already on the tip of her tongue. She stares at him in the face in complete disbelief, looks down at the cock for confirmation, and then goes back up to the face. He is surprised that she has turned around to face him, a look of exposure on his rugged face. They stare at each other for a moment, then at the cock that is as impressive in life as it was in Cadence's imagination. But it isn't Rajith's cock. The man standing in front of her is not Rajith.

She finally accepts that she has made a mistake, but it's too late. She knows, as she looks at the man before her that he will not leave her another note – for his own reasons. It dawns on her that this informant was nothing but a distraction, telling her things she already knew and dangling a rather impressive carrot in front of her, leading her down the wrong yellow brick road. Cadence accepts that she has wasted her time and commits to trusting nobody but herself from now on. This is her big break, London trusts her for the story, and she won't let them down.

The nameless stranger who isn't Rajith pushes her back against the wall and presses up against her. There's no point in letting the moment be lost now that the circumstance has been forfeited. Cadence had let her skirt fall back to just above her knee and it is now brought right back up around her waist. Her shaved pussy sweats from the heat outside it and drips from the heat inside of it. The sight of her cunt raises the cock immediately so that it hits against her clit as it reaches for the sky.

She wants him to fuck her now despite their location. It doesn't even matter that his cock will probably stretch her to capacity, making it a little difficult for her to get any real pleasure immediately, but after wasting her time, she decides to make the best of the situation. She will find what pleasure she can in the short time that she has already allocated in her head to this unexpected and unusual scenario. He needs to get his cock inside her quickly so that not a second more is wasted.

Cadence closes her eyes and searches for images of Rajith. As they fill her head, she takes hold of the cock, giving the rod a brief hand job to ensure that it is rock solid. She can't afford to let it die on her now. Lips fall onto her neck and she is again lost in a spicy forest, the scent all around her and inside her nose and head. She breathes it in and pulls on the cock that she is sure can now enter her tight little cunt with ease. It could probably enter any cunt, given its size and strength. She needs it inside her and tries to steer it in the right direction.

Before the head is in range of her pussy, she feels a thumb in her cunt, a middle finger inserted into her ass, dry. The sweat is the only moisture that aids her ass as the finger makes a full entry. Her cunt receives the thumb easily and simply augments her need for the cock. She pulls on the cock with both hands and raises herself onto her tiptoes as the fingers dig into her and move around inside her, the kisses on her neck a contrast between soft lips and not-so-soft beard. She can't imagine her cunt getting any wetter now and urges the man with his fingers in both her holes to fuck her.

Although the thought of a dry fuck in the alley is what had gotten her aroused, Cadence is now anything but dry. She tries again for the cock to align with her cunt, and again she is given nothing but a finger. The middle finger that was in her ass is now in her cunt. She is grateful for the added length and thickness. Also, with just one finger to focus on, her beaux can really do some work on her pussy. The finger makes quick entries and exits, in and out of the wet vagina. The heat inside the cunt arouses him even more, and he lets his finger soak it up every so often before resuming his brisk fingering.

This fuck will quite completely fuck up her investigation, making her informant completely redundant once his cock has been inside her. She reminds herself that he was of little value anyway, and she secretly hopes that there was nothing in him that might have been of use later. If he was holding out until later, wanting to enjoy his brazen flirtation, then she had now given herself to him too quickly and whatever he still had was lost. She makes the final call to attach his value instead to the experience she's about to have between the moment of his cock entering her and the moment of its final exit.

Thoughts of Rajith are filling her head again. His cock, not much unlike the one in her hands, is now her all-consuming thought. She can resist the urge to be fucked no longer. There has actually been no resistance. So what was the deal with the fingering? It was time to fuck and be done with it. The movement of people on the bridge above them makes Cadence both nervous and excited. There is no time for this teasing. She lines the missile up with her cunt for yet another attempt, trying to encourage the finger inside her to make the necessary accommodations. It just makes more insistent stabs into her cunt.

Cadence knows that if this fuck is fantastic, she will probably have no need to be fucked by Rajith, restoring her objectivity immediately. She's also a good-enough journalist to get the information she needs on her own or to find another informant. She knew better than to listen to an informant who sought her out. Such an elaborate distraction should have been obvious. But because of the heat, coupled with the realization that there was some pretty decent cock to be enjoyed in Mumbai, a young woman would be forgiven for letting her femininity get the better of her.

A few more digs from the finger and then Cadence has had enough. She pushes down on the hand and the finger slips out. The owner of the cock in her hand has to move back a little and get low as she pushes his cock down and then rests her vagina on its head. Immediately the dick disappears into her and the informant stands up as he makes further advancement. With his cock now in place, Cadence can do nothing but hope that he understands the urgency of the situation. Her cunt has graciously taken as much of him as would be possible on a good day in a better circumstance, so now it was up to him to make it work for both of them.

He plants his hands on the brick wall behind Cadence and fucks her hard into it. He starts to mumble something in her ear before he realizes that this is not necessary and his cock is the only reason Cadence still suffers his company. The thought forces him to focus on fucking her well for all her patience. He looks down to where his cock darts in and out of her, realizing that most of it is still to make the acquaintance of her vagina. He reaches under her thighs and lifts her off the ground so that she sits with one ass cheek on each of his palms and with her back against the wall. He watches again as his cock disappears into her, a further two or three inches this time.

It takes a few minutes of careful thrusting, solid fucking inwards and upwards, for him to max out his cunt pass. When she's finally taken all that she can in the new position, he sends solid thrusts into her as he lets himself start the race for climax. Deep in with just short lengths out, he impales the redhead to the wall. His fucking is a sweaty savagery that Cadence soon finds herself totally overwhelmed with. She doesn't try to shut herself up as the rod ploughs so far into her that she feels like she could easily suck his cock at the same time. The thought of his dick moving through her cunt and protruding out of her mouth is an exaggeration that serves her fantasy well, and she is soon sending rivers of her pussy lava over his mamba.

His fucking doesn't skip a beat. He even breaks into choruses of match fixing and what she should look out for going forward, all without breaking formation or missing a stroke. His cock shoots deep inside her and then pulsates to the rhythm of her beating cunt. Their motions come together in the sweltering heat along with their orgasms, and Cadence lets out a scream as she makes it rain all over the cock that has kept her off the ground for almost half an hour. A few more deep thrusts and a squeaky scream are what bring the cock out of her, and she watches as his load finds not only the back of the wall but also a large part of the ground a considerable distance away.

He squeezes on his cock until it stops spitting cream, pulls his pants up and his shirt down, and leaves her in the alley alone to sort herself out. She knows she will never see him again and so doesn't for a second allow herself to be embarrassed. She stumbles a little when she tries to make for the sunlight, a reminder that she was just solidly invaded by 14 inches of cock. It doesn't take too long for Cadence to gather herself though, and she showers and goes on her bed in her air-conditioned room within the hour. There can be no more distractions now, she tells herself as she allows herself to sleep.

The heat is unbearable at the match, but Cadence has a renewed focus. It feels like the beginning of a brand new day now that she has put the wasted efforts of her distraction behind her. The game is exciting enough for everyone, and it seems for a while that the Mumbai Masters have regained their form. The fans are ecstatic and the opposition is nervous. Everything seems to be going well. It all seems to be going a little too well and even Cadence starts to sit up and pay attention.

But halfway through the second half of the match, when it seems that nothing could possibly go wrong, the Mumbai Masters start to come undone. The mistakes they make are so obvious that even the coach appears livid as the camera catches him and his face is fed to the screen for the world to see. Fans are on their feet and the atmosphere in the stadium takes on a menacing air. This will be the third defeat for Rajith and his team, a third loss as a result of foolish mistakes, and it seems the supporters of the Mumbai Masters will have none of it. On home ground no less?!

Once the umpire calls the match, the

Masters cannot get off the pitch quickly enough as cans and other missiles are thrown at them from the stands. The crowd is angry and needs to be contained. The winners too make a quick escape and can barely enjoy the moment. Cadence is already at the manager's office, waiting for Vimal to finish up with the team. She needs to get some notion of the agenda of the team before she starts piecing her story together. She also needs to get proof of the fixing.

"This is not a good time, Cadence," Vimal is dismissive when he finally appears.

"Is there something you want to tell me, Vimal?" Cadence calls him out.

"What exactly are you insinuating, Miss?" Vimal plays for time.

"I'm saying that maybe there's something you want to share with me." Cadence isn't playing.

"You might want to go and look for stories elsewhere, and leave my team to process another defeat." He isn't budging.

The losing streak is a little too sudden for it to be coincidence. So if nothing else, Cadence knows that she is on to something. Also, the way Vimal deliberately dismissed her – and avoided her questions – and the way somebody went out of their way to send her on a wild goose chase, she is more determined than ever now to break the story. And she knows that she is very close to the source now. She goes back to her hotel room to regroup.

The knock on her door is unexpected. Even more unexpected is Rajith on the other side of it. She knows it's not a good idea to let him in, and so she fills the doorway with her tiny self and waits for him to let her know what he wants. He doesn't speak, giving her a long searching look instead. She returns the look, trying to figure him out for herself.

"You can't be here," she says.

"But here I am." He is his usual self.

She tries to resist him, stepping back into the room and closing the door. But he stops the door from closing completely with his foot, and she doesn't make another attempt to resist. Rajith closes the door himself once he has gotten inside, and Cadence walks straight to the window so that she can keep her composure. He throws his eyes on her notes but doesn't linger long enough to process anything. She draws his attention to her instead, knowing that this is no time to lose sight of the objective.

"We haven't been playing very well," Rajith admits.

"Deliberately?" Cadence checks.

"I don't follow," Rajith plays dumb.

"Never mind," Cadence lets him.

There is no need for Rajith to share some of the personal things he starts to tell Cadence, but she realizes that it's probably his way of making her understand why they're not doing so well. This might have passed her by if he was the reason why they were losing, but he wasn't. And despite the fact that Cadence isn't really an enthusiastic cricketer, her sports background makes her aware that it's highly unlikely for one person to have such an overwhelming effect on the performance of the entire team. But maybe he really is just feeling responsible, so Cadence humors him for a minute.

Unaware how he does it, Cadence is soon face to face with Rajith. Somewhere in the middle of his proclamations, he has managed to glide across the room to her. She doesn't have enough time to arm herself internally against his advances, and much to her delight and disappointment she finds her cunt moistening for the sheer proximity of her cunt to his cock. He's close enough for her to smell him now – really smell him. Memories of mammoth Mumbai cock fill her head and loosen her cunt, and she knows that the battle is lost.

As soon as Rajith sees the weakness in her eyes, he goes in for the kill. He pulls Cadence to him and wraps her legs around his waist without lifting her off the table she sits on. She leans back, her hands flat on the surface, her arms stretching behind her. Her breasts rise towards Rajith, who leans down to meet them. He stands back and parts her legs so that he can see the angle of entry available to him. It's going to be awkward at best. He pulls her a little more towards him so that only half of her butt remains on the wooden surface, her cunt and asshole handing precariously over the cliff formed by the end of the table.

Cadence uses her hands on the table and her legs against the sides of Rajith's thighs to keep herself up as his hands find her breasts over her tank top. He manages to bring them to a firm roundness, the thick nipples straining with desire beneath the fabric. Once her breasts have made the appropriate response, he lets his hands slip under the fabric of her top where there is no bra to keep his warm hands from her flesh. Rajith's hands on her force an arch out of Cadence that sees her breasts pushed up hard against his hands as they move around on them.

Her back is flat on the table, her legs in the air as Rajith removes her hot pants, then her panties. Her cunt is perfectly shaven, unusual for Rajith who is used to women with a little more hair. The pink flesh of Cadence's pussy has nowhere to hide as her legs are parted and the slit examined. Rajith's cock presses excitedly against his pants, also the kind unsympathetic to his bulge. Now that it is clear that this cock will enter her, Cadence is suddenly extremely aware of its size. She's aware that her cunt can handle size, but just how big is Rajith, his dick still not fully erect and still under cover.

He can't resist taking the pink in his mouth. The hair on his face tickles Cadence as the tongue in his mouth rattles her vagina. Her clit is enveloped completely and his tongue makes a fair effort at making the lips a part of the action. Then his thick dark tongue is inside her, shooting into her with the repetitive rattle of a large snake. He sings songs into her pussy, which responds by wetting the surface of the eager flesh so that it can continue to sing. Rajith enjoys eating her cunt with the enthusiasm of a first timer. Is it that perhaps the 25-year-old has not yet had the pleasure of clean-shaven cunt?

Her knees bend over his shoulders and her legs rest down his back as his head makes itself comfortable on her pussy. More and more she lets herself go as his enthusiasm for her cunt makes gains. He comes up a little and uses his fingers to part the lips so that he can look into her vagina. The white he finds near the entrance excites him even more, and he licks it up with his thick tongue, which is proving to be quite an ally. Again he examines the cunt, sending his finger in slowly, enjoying the finger's coated exit. The content of her pussy is sufficient to drive him insane.

Cadence looks down at his head, noticing that as he lifts it to examine her cunt again, he has pulled his pants down and that his dick is wrapped in a shiny blue condom. When had he done that? Had he come to her with the condom already in place? The assumption that she would be fucked by him offends her briefly. But then the sight of the fully erect cock so close to her tiny-by-comparison cunt makes his offense forgivable. It doesn't matter what his thinking was anymore because whatever it was, he was absolutely right. She lets it go and, in the process, herself.

Rajith times his entry perfectly. His cock slides smoothly into Cadence's cunt, her legs still perched on his shoulders. Even with its massive girth and the added squeeze from the position she's in, the movement of the dick in and out of her is fluid. He doesn't fuck her in the traditional back and forth motion that came down through evolution. He dips his cock into her in an almost up–down, sink-and-lift type of movement. Once inside her though, the cock follows the path of her pussy and makes its way to the back of her willing vagina, making contact with her G-spot on both the entry and the exit.

He lifts her effortlessly off the desk and moves her to the widow. The breeze cools the sweat on her skin and for fleeting moments, she is cold. The sensation is extremely welcome. The contrasts of hot and cold make her shiver slightly due to the unpredictability of the sensation. He holds her up until she's perched on the ledge and then feeds her six inches of his cock, adding to the four that stayed inside her during the move. The thick tool moves in and out of her with a force that makes her think she might fall out of the window. Rajith keeps firm hold of her legs to assure her that this won't happen.

Again, he lifts her up, her ass hanging above the ground while her cunt is suspended on his cock. He raises and lowers her over his dick as he paces around the room. Up and down she moves as Rajith takes her on a scenic tour of the room she hadn't really looked at before. The bed seems like the obvious place to be when Rajith's arms start to take a little strain. He makes his way to it while letting Cadence just sit on his cock for the short trip.

On the bed, Rajith fucks Cadence as though her cunt was getting in the way of his cock and the bed. He digs into her so hard that she gasps and has to ask him to take it easy. He lets his dick rest inside her until she starts to move around it. Taking the cue, he makes tentative thrusts into the tight hole and soon he is sliding thick inches into the redhead with the smooth cunt. His cock starts to voice its appreciation for the superbly maintained pussy, and the already thick dick grows to its maximum girth under the guidance of the English Channel it's invading.

He continues to fuck her, drawing more orgasms out of her than Cadence has had in a month. She's not tired. He's definitely not tired. They don't speak as their bodies do all the communication necessary. There is no sign of an end soon, and fortunately, both pussy and cock seem up to the challenge. Rajith makes slight changes to his dipping. Then he digs, then he dips, then he all out thrusts, and then he just lets his cock fill Cadence's cunt and allow her to do what she needs to do. There is never once the sense that the cock has any intention of leaving her cunt as the fucking continues with a steady determination.

It's past midnight and Rajith's cock is still rock solid, still inside her. The comfort of the bed seems to have given him renewed vigor, and he presses on. Cadence isn't complaining as her cunt is totally stuffed and every inch of her is attended to from the inside. The ripples sent through her entire body from the epicenter that is her cunt are mind-blowing. Rajith finally starts a series of low grunts. His orgasm has finally come along with her tenth. Or is it her twelfth? He sends his dick into her in tune with his grunts, and his final dig, almost through her, is coupled with a loud exhale and rivers of sweat from his hair. The slow extraction of his cock is necessary not just for Cadence's comfort but also because after such extensive fucking, Rajith has enough cum in the condom to put considerable pressure on it, the massive load risking explosion.

He takes care of the condom and his cock in the bathroom before returning to the bed with a towel for Cadence. He attends to her and then gets them both some drinks. They speak of nothing for a while and then drift off into the kind of post-fucking slumber that could easily last for days, or at least as long as it takes for the dick in the room to recover. Sleep comes easily but not completely, and the breeze dances over them as they try to snooze.

The note sliding under her door is unexpected. Cadence is on her way to the bathroom when she notices the shadow, then the piece of paper shortly after. The shadow disappears as she goes for the note. The writing on this note is different. This raises alarm bells for her, especially since it is telling her that there will be a payoff in about two hours at Vimal's office. Could it be a setup? She can't be sure. She won't be sure until she's been there. She goes to the bathroom, remembering her need.

On the bed, Rajith sleeps soundly. She looks at his cock, trying not to let it distract her. She starts to play out the various scenarios in her head, and so she e-mails her editor, telling him about the meeting, its location, and time. They make the necessary safety notification arrangements and Cadence starts to plan her exit. It's the middle of the night and she can't just disappear without an explanation to the man who just fucked her all ways and then some. She decides to play the only card she has.

With two hours before the meeting, she wakes Rajith, who's surprised that she has awoken him by taking his thick limp cock into her mouth. She sucks on the cock and is glad that she doesn't need to wait too long for a response. Rajith sends his cock into Cadence as she lies on her side and she works her cunt expertly around it so that this time it isn't long before she is raining onto his cock. Shortly after, Rajith removes his rod and cums all over Cadence's cunt and stomach. There is a moment shared, a smile, and then Cadence is in the bathroom.

"I'm not really a breakfast kind of girl," she says upon returning.

"I understand," Rajith has had his share of one-night stands to know that she doesn't want to wake up next to him.

He leaves without too much protest and Cadence immediately gets ready for her move. She gives him a chance to be gone in her mind, and even then she uses alternative exits, just in case. She steals through the city, appreciating the darkness and the silence despite some life in pockets that she passes. The training facility is closed up tight, and it takes everything she remembers from watching Nancy Drew for her to get into the facility without setting any alarms off.

The hall that gets her to Vimal's office is pitch black. She starts to wonder if this is a setup, but then voices make their way up to her through the darkness. She moves in closer, her tape already recording. She gets as close as she can and doesn't try to make out who is inside. She simply gets close enough so that every voice from inside the room is clearly captured on the recording device. It seems almost too easy, but everything that she had been hoping to gather was offered up to her, straight from the horse's mouths, in this one meeting. She hides in the shadows until she is sure everyone has left.

She gets back to the hotel with the adrenalin pumping through her. She knows that she should stay and maybe make a few mock interviews just to throw the team, but with what she heard on the tape, there is no time to play nice. This was going to get worse, and there were lives at stake. So the sooner arrests were made, the better. She calls the airport while listening to the tape for the last time and then transferring its contents to her laptop. She's going to e-mail it to London just as soon as the file has loaded. In the meantime, she packs. This trip was definitely worth it. There will be no regrets that she was sent to Mumbai, even though she seemed to luck her way through the trip. But what London didn't know couldn't hurt her, or her career.

It's almost 4 AM and the shadow under her door startles her. She anticipates a note. After a few minutes, there is nothing. She walks to the door, throws a look at her laptop, sees that the upload is still in progress, and then opens the door. Rajith stands in front of her, condoms in hand. He needs to get into the room, into her computer, and into her notes. Vimal's contact has given him the heads-up;

Cadence is on the first flight to London in the morning. Why so sudden? They need to know. It's too much of a coincidence that she wants to leave on the day they've received a massive payout and further plans have been made for future matches and the elimination of certain stumbling blocks.

The upload isn't very quiet and he throws an eye on her laptop. The words 'in progress' concern him, but he hides his concern behind his cock. "I couldn't sleep thinking about you." He tries charm.

"Can't get enough of fucking the English girl?" Cadence has other things on her mind but instinct tells her it would be best to play along.

"What do you think? One more round before dawn?" Rajith needs to get into the room.

She lets him in. Her flight is only at ten and she needs to wait for the upload to finish before she can e-mail it anyway. There's no way he can get to her laptop without her noticing, unless she leaves him alone in the room. She won't be leaving him alone. Suddenly she realizes the coincidence and sees the mission Rajith has been sent on. Another distraction it seems. So cock was how they thought journalists could be kept from doing their jobs. Rajith is here to get whatever proof she has, which means her recording isn't safe. But if his cock was to be his weapon, then her cunt was going to prove to be a worthy opponent. There would be no deleting of anything, not under the watch of her suddenly very energized vagina.

She pulls him straight to the bed, removing her own clothes so that she is totally naked by the time they're on the bed. He takes his clothes off sitting. She takes the condom from him and places it on the side of the bed. Cadence takes her own hand and covers her cunt as she straddles Rajith. She brings herself to a standing position and sends two of her fingers into her cunt while Rajith watches. His cock is a solid rod in seconds. He watches, salivating, as her fingers dig deeper and deeper into her and then come out, white. He pulls her to him and takes her fingers, then her pussy into his mouth.

Cadence parts her legs as soon as Rajith has drunk his fill. He watches as she takes his cock in her hand and guides the tip into her with little effort. She sits on the cock, ensuring that he sees his snake disappearing into her. The visuals harden his cock and soon she has it maxed out and her cunt takes the full force of the strain. She rides the cock that has managed to get inside her, and Rajith handles the part of his cock that cannot be accommodated. He moves his eyes from his cock, to her breasts, to the laptop on the table not a body length from where he is having his dick ridden.

He holds her on his cock and forces his dick further into her from below. She is practically lying on his chest as he rams her with his dick, holding her against him to avoid slippage. There is no chance of this as her cunt becomes increasingly more possessive of his cock. In and out of her his serpent slithers, her pussy greeting each entry with a complimentary welcome drink. There are moments where his cock bends on the outside of her cunt for the force with which he drives it into her. She makes the adjustment and takes enough of him into her to allow his dick to straighten out. Upon straightening, the fucking resumes forcefully.

Cadence raises herself back to sitting and then throws herself back gently so that she is on her back between Rajith's legs. He follows her up until he is sitting and then lifts her just so that he can get to his knees without removing his cock from her. She's soon on her back again, her legs held in the air and apart by a revitalized Rajith who sends all of himself into her from above. The aerial assault results in an almost complete penetration and Cadence is again forced to raise the white flag. Rajith gives her a few inches of relief, no more, and proceeds with his task of fucking her.

Her cunt is generous with its moisture and Rajith is generous with his cock. He keeps driving it into her as she creates the slippery environment that makes it possible. Her cunt pulls so much of the cock into itself that even when the cock loses some firmness, it goes by unnoticed. Rajith simply rams his dick in and out of her until enough of her cunt juice is on the outside of her, restoring the original interior state of her cunt, which results in solid cock. The stiff dick is then driven into her in long hard strokes, deep enough to draw another river, striking oil at regular intervals now so that the system they've developed becomes a comfortable pattern. It is in this comfort zone of cock and cunt that they both come to an incredible climax.

Rajith is careful about ensuring that Cadence is asleep as he slips out of the bed. He makes for the laptop, checking the whole time that she doesn't stir. Every time he gets to the laptop she stirs, sending him into a light panic and stopping him dead in his tracks. She resumes her sleeping and he decides to just go to the bathroom. He'll have to look out for another opportunity to get rid of the evidence. Back in bed, he tries in vain to stay awake and is soon snoring louder than he would have had if he had gotten a little more sleep.

Cadence stirs completely at the sound of his snoring. It isn't incredibly loud, but anyone accustomed to the sound of their own breathing and nothing else is bound to stir. She's certain that he is more asleep than she was, and she goes for the gap. It takes her less than thirty seconds to e-mail the file and double-check that it has been backed up. She returns the screen to its original state and makes for the bathroom. Cadence wants to sleep now and so she needs Rajith to get his assignment over with. She drops the toothpaste into the sink and turns the tap on.

The water and the sound of Cadence brushing her teeth are not what wake Rajith. Her absence from the bed does. He knows he has less than a minute and so it takes him as long to delete the uploaded file and also to tape static over the tape in the recorder. He leaves the screen as he found it and makes for the bed. The tap closes and so do Rajith's eyes. He can't fake sleep and so he hides his head in the pillows. The breeze coming through the window is warming up as the sun starts to make its appearance in the distance.

Cadence throws herself face down on the bed, wanting to wake Rajith. He turns to face her. Her eyes are on him. "What's up?" he asks, trying to sound like he's been woken up, failing to. Cadence gets onto her knees and parts her legs. Rajith is behind her almost instantly. He checks for moisture and finds none. He uses his own saliva to moisten the entrance while he rolls the condom down his shaft with the other hand. She grabs onto the brass headboard as he inserts his cock into her. She pushes herself into him so that the entry is quick. Rajith is soon fucking the shit out of her little cunt as the sun enters the room, offering up rays of good morning, while Rajith brings themselves to the first of two orgasms.

For the second climax, Cadence rides the shit out of him, knowing that his team will be in very hot water shortly and so the least she can do is to give him the fuck of his life since she has already sailed his team down the river without the proverbial paddle. She has succeeded, as she knew she would, in letting Rajith believe that he has won. She knows that the file has been sent and also that the original has been backed up to a remote server. So for the rest of the time she is in Mumbai, a few hours at best, she takes the full measure of Rajith into her and allows herself to be repeatedly bowled over by the unsuspecting wicketkeeper.

3 CARMANITA'S COURAGE

The gypsy women move the way they sing. Even under their layers of clothing, they are obviously beautifully built. As they walk behind the horses of the warriors who've just burnt their wagons to the ground, driven their men away, and taken them captive, they seem to glide over the earth. Their breasts are covered by waves of raven hair, and when they pull it aside to wipe the sweat from their chests, very few of the warriors manage not to look. The rest simply give the alluring mounds the once-over.

It becomes obvious very quickly once they arrive at the camp that the men have no intention of having sex with the women they think of as nothing more than cursed witches. The women will simply keep the camp clean and the men fed. Gypsy women are famous for being hardworking and being able to do everything from hunt and skin a wild boar to start a fire and create a shelter. So they're the perfect slaves for the warriors, who are usually too tired after a battle to do any of these things to any real standard. So the gypsy bitches will do this for them, giving the warriors the joy of dealing the women the added insult of having them, these women who loathe them and who call them barbarians, cleaning up after them.

Carmanita is one of the youngest captives, just twenty years old. She has wisdom that surpasses even her beauty. Her intuition is always right and she has often given valuable advice to the older women in the group in the days before they were captured. Carmanita seems most to understand men. She has a sense about them that belies her years, and she has never been wrong when she's passed judgment or a comment. Even now, captured, she encourages the others, assuring them that everything will be okay. She bands them together and helps them just get on with things. This attracts attention to her and she is soon singled out for the taunts of the men, who accuse her of trying to incite a revolt.

It's during their bathing times that Carmanita and a few of the other younger women realize that while the warriors might call them witches, they still see them as women. Every day, as the sun sets and the women make their way to the nearby stream to bathe, they are escorted by at least a dozen more men than are necessary. The rest conspicuously find perches from which they can observe the nymphs in the water. The gypsy women realize that it might not be too difficult after all to escape this hell, provided they utilize the one thing they didn't know was actually at their disposal: the lust of the men who have captured them.

The sun hangs its usual low as the day begins to give way to the night. The evening fires are already ablaze and the smell of dinner rises from the large pots from which the men will serve themselves after the women have eaten. This isn't courtesy of course but just a precaution against poisoning. After all, the reality of the situation hangs in the air as a constant, an ever-present indicator of the reality of the circumstance.

Carmanita is the first one into the water, followed by the others as they wash up before dinner. The men find a spot on the banks and busy their hands with tasks that don't require the participation of their eyes. Their eyes are on the women in the water. Nothing but their undergarments on, they all start to cup water in their hands and run it down their breasts, then their backs. They wet themselves this way, almost ritualistically. Carmanita has a new ritual today though. She catches several eyes on her and waits for a few more. She wants to maximize the effect of what she is about to do, and so she patiently waits for those not looking in her direction to do so. She doesn't wait very long....

She pulls her undergarment lower than it's ever been over her breasts so that one more tug will expose her ripe nipples. She then lets herself drop completely into the water, disappearing beneath the surface. Slowly she reemerges, the undergarment clinging to her tightly, her nipples clearly visible through the light white fabric. She throws her head to the side slowly, allowing every ray of the sun that dares linger too long to catch her every move. The sunlight turns her into an amber goddess. Her hair falls in a million curls around her face and she leaves it there. She pauses briefly, allows for the stares, and then slowly pushes her hair to the back.

Suddenly everyone is watching her. Even the other women seem to be mesmerized by her. She lifts the skirt of her undergarment over her knees, then above her thighs, tucking it in at her hips so that it stays up. This augments her figure, accentuating every curve. In a modest gesture, she turns to the side slightly and then lets the fabric fall down her shoulders and down past her breasts so that they are completely exposed now. She lets them be warmed in the remaining sunlight, ever so slightly out of view of everyone else.

There is an almost audible anxiety, as she seems to turn towards her audience. Everyone braces themselves for the visuals they anticipate. But by the time Carmanita is again square against the crowd, she has returned the fabric to her shoulders and her breasts are covered. The skirt of her undergarment is untucked and it falls into the water, almost floating on top of it as she makes her way to the shore towards the men who now have significant bulges in their pants, bulges they are unable to hide for their own tight trousers.

The other gypsy women follow her out of the water, still stunned, still mesmerized. They look like a band of sylphs following their queen from the river. The sun has finally given in to the night and the orange glow from the fires catches the exodus from the lake. The men make the necessary adjustments to their dicks, as, for the first time, it is not gypsy witches that emerge from the lake but women. And they have no choice but to admit to themselves that in that moment, these women are in fact incredibly beautiful.

There are whispers around the gypsy fire as the women dry themselves. For the first time, the men have even forgotten the true dynamic of the situation, and some of them are already eating by the time the gypsies arrive and fill their own plates. The men eat in silence, not daring voice what thoughts run through their minds. Everyone is sure they are the only ones who dare to entertain the thought of fucking a witch and yet they all know that there wasn't a single limp dick on that riverbank. Carmanita and the others eat under the closest watch they have received since the first night they were captured.

The women fall asleep by the fire at the center of the camp. They are surrounded by warriors who sleep less soundly the further they are from the center. The watchers are always furthest from the fire, furthest from the warmth that might lull them to sleep. But none of the men are asleep. All of them are hoping that every other man is asleep. They look around for an opportunity to steal one of the women away into the woods or under the cover of the willows by the water. They all long to feel the fires that must burn between the thighs of their captives. But the opportunity evades them.

One woman is not asleep. She feels the

pierce of stares more than any of the others do. This isn't surprising since she initiated this entire situation. She is the one who reminded the men that they had in fact captured women and not animals. And because of Carmanita's actions, there was now, for the first time, the chance that the women would be turned into sex slaves as well. But she knew better, having an understanding of the way people thought of gypsies, the manner in which they processed rumors in their heads. Carmanita wasn't playing a careless game. She knew exactly what she was doing. And if she was going to succeed, she would have to be very careful whom she let in on the plan....

Razar is the leader of the warriors that have captured the gypsies. They're a small army, surviving on their plundering really, as nomadic as the gypsies, and so their dislike for them is a little irrational. They call themselves soldiers of the liberation; but with no liberation struggle underway and every tribe and village living largely independent existences, many see Razar's army as nothing more than a band of bullies. They're not really bad men, just habitual soldiers who've become bored with peace.

Carmanita finds herself in Razar's tent, surrounded by Razar and four of his generals. Each general leads one of the four camps that make up the little army. They are all aware that she is up to something and that this has a lot to do with the flaunting of her sexuality in front of the soldiers she knows to be sex-starved. The purpose of this meeting is to put a stop to it, whatever it is, before the gypsy causes any real trouble.

"There are a lot of angry cocks in this camp because of you," Razar addresses Carmanita directly.

"Why angry? Surely there is no desire to plant these cocks into a band of witches?" Carmanita is bold.

The generals break into an almost singular chorus as Carmanita's boldness confirms their suspicions. They start to speak over each other, all trying to be heard. They want to be sure that Razar now sees that they were right to be concerned about the agenda of the gypsy. He silences them and then gives Carmanita a long stare, questioning her with his eyes, her own eyes locked with his.

"There are many other tribes nearby that are not as selective over where it is they plant their cocks. You might want to remember that before you start stirring fires you are not able to put out." Razar's warning is clear. The others are happy that he has made their point. Carmanita knows only that her plan is already working. The men in the camp are coming loose for all the sexual tension she has created.

The five dicks in the room strain in the trousers that cover them as Carmanita throws her head back slightly and lets the full length of her neck be appreciated. She turns to leave without being excused and sways her hips in mock defiance as she exits, sure that every eye in the room is on her. Her own thoughts are filled with the words Razar spoke. Surely, would he sell off a supply of exotic cunt that he himself could enjoy? She hopes not as she makes her way down to the river, the others in tow. If he could, then her plan has no hope of success.

As the water starts to make its way up their thighs, there is a moment where they doubt, where even Carmanita doubts. But then they remember their current lives and their past lives and wade deeper and deeper into the river. Carmanita knows that all eyes are now on her and she knows the threat made by Razar was real. But even so, she doesn't want to stay with these men longer than she needs to, and she wants the other women who have lost lovers and husbands to the wilderness to be able to get back to them before both heart and spirit are lost. There is just nothing to it. She knows what needs to be done.

In the water Carmanita starts her ritual, her skirt completely discarded this time, floating a little way down the river for a while before one of the others catches it. She lets the fabric of her undergarment cling to her for a moment before lifting it to her waist and tucking it high above her thighs. Everyone watching knows that her legs are exposed under the water, her cunt naked to the gentle current. This knowledge has everyone looking at her with intent despite the fact that all they can see is half of her from her waist up that isn't submerged.

There is an immediate sense that the soldiers are not so much aroused as they are upset. And why wouldn't they be, teased so blatantly by women they should technically be able to have but whom they cannot have because of their own very loud disdain of the bitches they now have to admit are actually very attractive. Everyone but Carmanita shows the fear that they feel at the stares they are getting. It's time for the biggest gamble so far. All eyes are on Carmanita in anticipation of her next move. Every soldier, every man is on the riverbank, watching to see if she dares play tease in spite of Razar's warning.

Suddenly Carmanita lifts her covering over her head and stands naked in the afternoon that has become a moonlit evening. Her nudity has the entire situation suspended, despite the fact that it is her silhouette that suggests her nakedness in the dim light, nothing more. Fear, anxiety, and apprehension fuse in the night air as Carmanita lets her hands move over her naked self, her breasts reaching out in front of her and almost up as the nipples make their acknowledgment of the chill. She is lost repeatedly under the water in spite of the cold, each time emerging with larger, rounder, harder breasts. Her hands are on her chest in a mock attempt to warm them up and clean them. For the duration of what has become some serious fondling, nobody else in the water bathes, and none of the soldiers move.

The sun has set too soon for the soldiers as they strain to see what it is exactly that Carmanita is doing to herself. She is so deliberate about her touching that despite the only light coming from the moon reflecting on the surface of the water, there is no doubt when her fingers are on her vagina, no question of when it is that she lets her own delicate little fingers stray into her pussy, wet from the outside. For the briefest moment the scene is allowed to play out, just long enough for the men watching to realize that they have been bewitched, their cocks now hanging outside of their trousers, their hands pulling on their throbbing meat, some of the rods dripping some serious semen. Suddenly four, then five men, more, are in the water, pulling Carmanita from what she had mistakenly thought to be a safe stage for her little performance. A moment later, every one of the gypsies is around their fire, naked, the soldiers ogling them as they eat.

The light from the fires licks up the tanned bodies, every woman cupping her breasts as opposed to hiding her exposed pussy. To everyone's shock Carmanita immediately touches herself again in full view now of the men. There is nothing to hide her fingers as they trace over her breasts, down her sides, onto her stomach and then down, deep between her thighs. She lets her fingers circle her clit until it starts to swell. The growing arousal sends an odor into the air that permeates even that of the meat the soldiers are eating, and it isn't long before all their plates are discarded. It seems like the men might descend upon Carmanita at any moment, and what they will do to her is as clear as the slender finger now dancing somewhere in, somewhat out of her vagina.

With all the sensuality they can muster through their fear, the others quickly follow suit. Their own hands are on their cunts quickly, tickling their abundant curls, finding the pink pearl beneath the black. The clitorises start to bloom, emitting the same erotic odor as Carmanita's. The scent of pussy hangs in the air, thick enough for the soldiers to be floored by it. They don't stand anymore, reclining now with their free fingers fondling firm fuck sticks. There is nothing about the scene that suggests that it will end in anything other than one huge motherfucking orgy. It threatens to be savage.

The tension rises quickly. It's not clear anymore what the women expect to happen, but what is clear is that the men are as aroused as they need to be to be forgiven for whatever it is they do next. They have no care anymore that the women who parade their dripping cunts in front of them are their captives, witches caught to cook and clean. They see only naked women whose pussies are wet and ready for swift and immediate penetration. The entire camp seems to make a steady advance towards the women touching themselves around the roaring fire.

Curses start to spew from the soldiers' mouths as one by one they are off the ground, walking towards the women, cocks in hand. The women are oblivious to this as they are now completely lost in the frenzy of their collective masturbation. The soldiers get closer and closer to them, the women not even aware of how close as they dig deeper and deeper into themselves. While many of the women fuel their self-manipulation of their genitalia with imaginings of lovers lost, there are a few who have designs on the very men approaching them. But there is no way that the gypsy women would actually initiate a fuck with these barbarians. It's no longer clear if the barbarians feel the same way.

The soldiers are on the women just as some of them start to climax. The orgasms are loud enough to draw Razar and his generals from the tent in which they were eating. The scene has them stunned. The soldiers are pulling the women's fingers from their cunts, arresting their orgasms and sending their own fingers into them. Their larger, thicker, firmer fingers then bring the gypsies to additional orgasms, two men – sometimes three – on one woman. The men without cunts to play with are pulling on their cocks and shooting load after load on the naked bodies in front of them. There is no time to register anything but lust as Razar and his generals immediately scout the scene for the initiator of this display.

The bodies seem to intertwine, one into another, and so it is hard to tell where one ends and another begins. The euphoria has some of the women so dazed that they fall asleep despite the fingers moving around in their juiced-up cunts. The soldiers are unconcerned with whether the owners of the pussy they are working on are aware of them or not, just needing to feel for the secrets they need to discover inside the incredibly tight, incredibly hot vaginas. The women are as hot inside as the fire is outside, their skin a warm inviting tapestry for what could be incredible fucking.

Every soldier is pulling his cock, some at the sheer sight of the women, some at the feel of the wet heat inside of their pussies. That there is suddenly a desire to fuck them is not doubted, and the women are doing nothing to dissuade this desire. The soldiers let their hands do what they would like to be done by the vagina around them, hoping that their own climax will remove the desire to fuck these witches. Soon the men are cumming again, shooting their final loads over the women, some of the sleeping girls waking up at the touch of the hot liquid dropping onto them.

Finally, Razar spots Carmanita and instructs the generals to steal her away. A moment later, she's naked in his tent with her hands still skirting over her cunt, which drips, but only just. She hasn't yet cummed. The two men holding her pull her hands away from her pussy, aware that they are frustrating her efforts at climax. She didn't realize how badly she wanted to cum until she was hindered from doing so. Razar stands in front of her, flanked by the other two generals in the room. All five men have very large, very conspicuous erections.

Razar takes his fingers and pinches Carmanita's clit gently. She gives him a defiant look, trying her best to hide the fact that his touch has sent a million sensations through her body that she has never felt before. His eyes suddenly go from cold to a warm, piercing hazel. She is suddenly aware of his face, the strength of its structure, and the perfect placement of the nose, lips, and eyes on it. Even under the scruffy hair on his face, his lips are most inviting: pink, thick, and fleshy, parting to reveal the whitest teeth, the canines somewhat exaggerated.

For the first time she sees him as a man. She sees him as a very handsome man. And as his fingers bring her cunt to bloom, she becomes more of a woman to Razar than she has ever been. There is nothing that she can do to hide that her body is responding favorably to what is happening to her. And this is good for Razar, whose erection is the largest and most visible in the room. In fact, four inches of his cock have escaped the top of his pants and his thick dick head oozes cum over the swollen mushroom. The sight of this has Carmanita so aroused that she starts to ooze cunt juice herself, turning up the sexual tension in the room considerably. It's now clear that every man in the room wants to fuck her.

Carmanita realizes that her plan might be working too well. She was supposed to build up the tension, get the men ravaged by lust in the knowledge that they would never bypass superstition, and fuck them so that hopefully the tension would become unbearable and the witches would be driven away and replaced by more fuckable slaves. But now it seems that the men have bypassed superstition and that every cunt now was at risk of ravaging. This was not looking very good, given that the ratio of cocks to cunts was easily ten to one. Razar again lets her know, in a husky whisper, that he cannot be held responsible now for what could happen.

Everyone knows that it's too late though: every soldier outside has just one thing on his mind. And now that they have had their fingers inside the beautiful smoking cunts of their prisoners, it was only a matter of time before they give their cocks a taste of the pussy their fingers are now a little more familiar with. The look on Carmanita's face gives some indication even through the pleasure that she appreciates the concern, but this doesn't stop her from drawing a very dangerous comparison between the men around her and outside and the gypsy men who now wander around the wilderness, convinced that their women have been defiled by barbarians. Carmanita lets it be known that gypsy men have never left a gypsy woman unsatisfied. The challenge is heard loud and clear.

If there was ever the hope that the sexual frustration would drive the men mad, it is soon realized. Razar's response to Carmanita's taunt elevates the game so quickly that even the wiser-than-her-years Carmanita is suddenly left wondering what the hell she was thinking to put everyone in this position. Razar drags her outside and repeats her taunt, loud enough for him to be heard by every man and every woman. He says it in the same taunting, challenging tone as Carmanita had and then, after letting the challenge sink in, drags Carmanita back into his tent, followed by the four generals.

The soldiers look around at each other, then at the naked women, then back to one another. Is this a dare that they can't fuck as well as gypsy men? Are they perceived to be inadequate for these witches and seen as incapable of satisfying their cunts? If their fingers seem to have done a good enough job of bringing them to several orgasms, what more their cocks? These men have healthy, large dicks, able to fuck the best of pussy. They know from memory that they've left many satisfied women in their wake. Why now would they need to prove to these bitches that they could fuck as well, if not better than, their gypsy men? But the challenge had been made.

The question that hangs now is who will be the first to actually send his dick into one of them. Who would dare fuck a gypsy, a woman who'd been fucked by what Carmanita had described as a very virile gypsy man? It's not insecurity that begs the question but the fear that once the cumming was concluded, all who fucked the witches would be seen to be cursed, or tainted. But if they all fucked them, then there would be nobody left to judge. The problem is just that there were not enough cunts to go around, at least not all at once. Someone would have to go first – a few maybe, but still not everyone. And that was the problem.

In Razar's tent, he stares her down. Carmanita throws her eyes on every man in the room, avoiding Razar as long as possible. He pulls her to him, his hand immediately on her cunt. He wriggles his hand around between her thighs to part her legs, and when she resists, two generals pull her legs apart. The other two keep her from falling over. Razar then takes a dry index finger and feels for her hole. Finding it, he starts a slow entry into Carmanita's now dry vagina. Every few millimeters he pulls out some of his finger before making more advancement, still slowly as though he doesn't want to miss a thing.

After what seems like forever, he stops. Razar lets his fingertip feel around a little more and then push gently into her cunt, not too hard. He tests the back of her pussy for a while, moistening the cunt considerably. Despite the added moisture though, Razar's finger goes no further. He knows from his own considerable experience that if he pushed his finger any deeper, any harder, he would, upon withdrawing his finger, expose Carmanita as the one thing the situation didn't require her to be, the last thing her behavior would have suggested that she was: a virgin!

Razar pulls his finger from her and gives her a knowing look. He dismisses the generals without looking at them. They hesitate and his tone becomes a little more insistent. The generals leave reluctantly, their noses aware of Carmanita's fresh smell, their eyes on her wet cunt. She looks and smells like the first peach in spring, ready to be bitten. Hers looks like the kind of peach that will drip rivers down the chin of whomever is privileged enough to bite into it. Razar seems to be assuaging this privilege and is soon alone in the room, discussing Carmanita's virginity with her eyes in total silence.

The generals are aware that what they witnessed, the resistance to the finger, and the jackpot look on Razar's face could mean only one thing. And suddenly it seems unfair that their leader would be alone in deflowering the tease. The idea of violating the virgin consumes the four as they walk out onto a scene that only fuels their desire for a fuck even further. But unlike the gentle progression of the erotic scene before them, the generals have a more savage kind of fucking in mind.

Whether it is because of her defiance, her cheek, or her blatant disregard for them, the generals have it in their heads to taste the virgin, but not in the tender way required by virginity. They want to fuck her hard, and they want to fuck her at the same time. They want to confirm for her that everything she has ever heard about them is true. They also want her to know once and for all that they are as capable of fucking as any man she has ever lied about knowing. The generals' egos demand that they pay her back for her behavior. But for the moment, she is in the safety of Razar's tent, if he hasn't already gone ahead alone and taught her all these things.

Far from it though. Razar, at last speaking with his mouth, gives Carmanita a stern reprimand for putting herself at so much risk. He explains the importance of her virginity, of any virginity, and how they would never have even considered violating them like that until she made the thought so irresistible. Carmanita is speechless as she realizes that she played the game too well, and from the silent tension outside, the women were about to become containers for every cock in the camp. Carmanita is suddenly sad, a tear down her face letting this be known. Razar cannot speak as he realizes that she has come too to the realization of just what it is that she has done.

Outside the soldiers are starting to succumb to lust – but not only the soldiers but also the women too. There are little groupings that start to form as brief discussions reveal who is prepared to be fucked and who isn't. Those who don't really fancy the thought of being devoured by the soldiers are going to use the scene around them to fuel their own delivery of pleasure to their own cunts. Some of the soldiers, the ones with weaker stomachs, are drawn to these women, who will allow them to touch and to fondle them while taking care of their own cocks. The others find themselves at a stalemate as superstition hangs a heavy curtain between the cocks and cunts wanting to connect.

A delicious gypsy girl called Layla finds herself between two soldiers. The men, Cane and Seth, are tall, not much older than Layla, both of them in their early twenties and at a similar level of sexual experience – not virgins but also not experts. The men start to kiss the sides of Layla's face as her hands move over their bare chests. None of the men are brave enough yet for her mouth despite the appeal of her strawberry lips. Layla doesn't mind, aware of who and what they might still subconsciously think she is.

As their hands move over each other's bodies, everyone watches, almost expecting Layla to turn the men into toads or stone. But the more passionate the three become, the more the audience starts to be drawn in to the scene, all their predispositions and naïve expectations discarded. They now cast aside everything they've ever allowed themselves to hold as true, and allow themselves to enjoy the moment completely. Seth and Cane gently get Layla down to the ground, their blanket a soft covering on the already soft earth. Her legs are parted slightly as finally mouths are on mouths, the sweetness of Layla tasted by both men for the first time. The heat from the fire is on her thighs immediately and her cunt starts to pulsate deep inside, warming itself up.

Cane's fingers are inside her first. It's the hottest pussy he's ever been inside. The full length of his index dances around inside her hot place in a kind of delirium that would suggest a fever. Layla grabs onto Seth as Cane's finger sends her into a highly charged frenzy, unexpected since the three of them had thought they would take the cautious approach. Cane makes space for Seth's fingers as Seth sees that there is something inside Layla worth exploring. It takes seconds for his own fingers to experience the same delirium as Cane's.

The men dance inside her with their fingers. Her heat consumes them both as they alternate appendages and then enter her together. As her pussy starts to drip liquid heat, Layla holds on to both of them, watching as they draw more and more juice from the inside of her vagina. They fuck her with their fingers, hard and firm, then slow and gently. They contemplate whose dick will enter her first while they enjoy her cunt, knowing in their heads that their cocks will have the time of their lives inside her. But looking around, nobody else seems to be making any progression towards fucking. It seems that Seth and Cane will either set the tone or become the first to be ostracized for planting their cocks in a witch. But given the position of hands on bodies, cocks and cunts, everyone around them is just waiting for the first cock to find the inside of a pussy, and then they'll all follow suit.

It dawns on Seth and Cane that the best thing to do might be to go at it together. They communicate mostly using hand signals and eyes as their dicks become decidedly harder at the realization that they've come to an acceptable way forward. Cane's lips are on Layla's as she is turned on her side so that her body faces him completely. Seth gets up close behind her and then borrows her face from Cane so that his mouth can also settle on Layla's lips, drawing the warm sweetness from inside it with a long kiss.

Seth places his hand between her thighs from the back, lifting her leg so that she has to rest it over Cane's body in front of her. Cane pulls her into him a little more, Seth moving in closer, kissing her back and gently massaging her ass as he lets his cock rest on her inner thigh. Cane's cock is alongside Seth's, both on her thigh, the heads pointing in the general direction of her moist vagina. Both of them try for a grip on their dicks so that they can guide them into Layla steadily.

But the size of their fingers makes this difficult. So Cane, in the better position because he is facing Layla and has a better view of her cunt, takes both cocks in his large hand, squeezing them just enough at the head so that the two large dick heads merge slightly. Seth waits for Cane to get their cocks past the entrance, just the tip of their tips inside her, before moving himself closer so that his hipbone is against Layla's ass.

The inside of Layla's cunt is unmistakable as the heat is suddenly around the cocks. Both men are instantly aware that they've made entry and Cane immediately removes his hand from the dicks. Both men thrust forward simultaneously, cock against cock as they send ten inches of their respective cocks into her beautiful vagina. It takes them a few slow strokes to get the sensation to register; to accept that their dicks are rubbing against each other inside the hottest pussy either of them has ever had. But once this happens, they proceed to double-fuck her with the most intense passion and also the most decided precision they can muster, given that all they want to do is to shoot off their first loads in anticipation of the next round, a round they know will last longer.

They know that they will be able to give her cunt a more solid run after the first load is shot and so they speed up to the end. Layla doesn't pay too much attention, not really minding, knowing from past fucks with other more experienced men that her cunt is unusually heated and that it takes at least the first round for any cock, despite its size or experience, to acclimatize. Bigger dicks, thicker meat, have always had a better chance against the super-heated pussy though. So she lets the two men do what they need to, and in a few minutes, both of them have shot their first loads. Her cunt is now a slippery playground and they are both comfortable enough giving it a go solo.

Seth is left behind inside Layla as Cane withdraws first, his cock having gone slightly limp first even though it is the thicker meat. Layla rolls onto her stomach so that Seth is on top of her, sending his full strength into her from behind, as she rests her head on her hands and enjoys his powerful thrusting, the rest of the camp watching intently, enjoying the show thoroughly. Seth doesn't fuck her hard because he wants to hurt her or prove anything. He fucks her hard because there is no other way to fuck her. Layla's cunt is hotter than the fires of hell, and to leave a cock inside it stationary for even a second could result in a lost erection. So Seth pounds her pussy hard, the pleasure of it evidenced by her loud moans and pleas for more.

Cane answers the call, his cock rock solid by the time Seth shoots off his second load. Seth is barely off her when he is on her; his chest against her back as she maintains the position Seth had her in. She relaxes onto the softness of the blanket and the earth underneath her as Cane's rod finds her cunt and makes its way inside it. Cane's thrusts are quick as well, but not as Seth's were. He has a thicker cock and so he seems to be fucking her slower because of the pressure of his meat, which is now at full strength. He plants his hands on either side of her, needing the added impetus to drive his dick into her completely. Again, Layla is begging for more. Again and again, Cane delivers more with every stab.

The other men start to pull the women closer, parting the legs of the ones expressing the desire to be fucked. They're gentle about penetrating, ensuring first that the women are wet and willing. Fingers find pussies first, teasing, tugging, and moistening. The women help the men along by stroking their cocks, keeping them long, thick, and hard, while the men focus on preparing their pussies. The efforts pay off quickly as cunt after fuckable cunt becomes ready for cock. The sound of Cane's climax, a loud emphatic roar, sends the men into overdrive as they start to send cock after cock into the warm exotic cunts that have the entire lot of them in a trance.

Layla's cunt invites her beaus in once more, again both of them inside her at the same time. This time though she sits on Seth's long tool while Cane drives his thicker tool into her from above. They fuck her this way for several orgasms as the others try to draw the responses from their women that Seth and Cane manage repeatedly from Layla. The women are more capable though of drawing successive orgasmic roars from them as they use their vaginas to turn the cocks inside them into the only part of the men that exists for either of them for the longest time. There is not a moment when there isn't a cock in someone as the secrets of gypsy pussy reveal themselves over and over again.

Cane and Seth can't help a few more solo rides, Layla changing only her position, the temperature of her cunt remaining constant. They shoot massive loads as she brings them, one at a time, to final explosive orgasms, herself too. She reclines, half on her back, as she takes a much-needed break from the cocks that have taken all the tension of the past while and sent it to the moon. The men each keep a hand on some part of her body as an indication that nobody else gets to send their cocks into her. They fall asleep, but only slightly, flanking their cunt protectively as she rests up for the next session. The three recover in silence.

The rest of the camp becomes an orgy, everyone touching, fucking, and sucking. There isn't a dry cunt in the entire compound and very few limp cocks. The limp ones aren't limp for very long as the massive orgy plays out for the entire night, dissipating slowly at dawn. The generals have watched the scene, unable to involve themselves for their entire obsession with a certain virgin. They've pulled on their cocks and cummed a few times by their own hand, but not a cock amongst them has seen inside of a cunt. But now, as the sun comes up over the camp, they wonder what it is that has happened in Razar's tent and whether or not what is left will be at their disposal.

Carmanita leaves Razar's tent just as the sun confirms the arrival of the day. She gives the scene outside the once-over and realizes that everything has played out as she had feared; there's been some serious fucking! But the others quickly assure her that there was not a single moment that was unpleasant. Everyone wants to know what happened between her and Razar, and when she says nothing, it is for a while before they start to believe her. The more experienced women know that she is still a virgin though, something in the sway of her hips and her unknowing eyes. The whispers of her virginity flutter through the entire camp, if nothing but to confirm that Razar, like most of his soldiers, is really not that bad. These whispers reignite the desire, the absolute obsession with Carmanita's virginity, the four generals very pleased that their leader is more of a gentleman than they are.

Some of the others who've been awake long enough to have been to the river and back are already making love, fresh bodies locked in heated embraces. There is no indication of breakfast as everyone who isn't fucking is still sleeping. Carmanita watches as the women are handled with the most delicate hands, the utmost care as cocks move in and out of them only at their request. There is a lot of kissing and a lot of fondling, the sensuality of the morning making Carmanita wish suddenly that Razar was somewhat less of a gentleman. The smell of sex quickly fills the early morning air.

A tiny nymph, Tamar, is hardly five feet. She finds herself in the solid grip of a bearish giant, Gore, a massive tree of seven feet. The lithe beauty is naked beside the hairy beast who kisses every part of her with the gentlest lips, the hair on his face tickling her delicate bronzed skin. He moves her raven waves from her breasts and sucks so gently on the mounds that Tamar may as well be suckling a newborn baby. The impossibility of the two of them draws everyone's attention, and soon enough even those sleeping are now throwing interested eyes in the direction of the gypsy beauty and her beast.

There is no shame or no embarrassment despite the audience and the full exposition made possible by the sun as Tamar and Gore lose themselves in one another. Gore's naked body is covered almost completely in orange hair, a stark contrast to his milk-white skin. Tamar is darker, an almost golden against his ivory. His cock is thick, long, and uncircumcised. There are easily eighteen inches of meat. It looks like twenty but that just seems impossible. There is enough of his foreskin to hang over the head despite the cock being fully erect. The head of his penis under the soft flesh is the same girth as the rest of the cock, except for a slight widening at the base of the head, which quickly narrows to become the same girth as the tip again.

Tamar pulls the skin back off the cock head and then pulls it back over the monster. Her gentle fingers are quick to draw milk from the python, liquid she licks up with her tiny tongue as though from it she would draw the strength necessary for the rest of the cock. Gore sits with his legs crossed as she tongues his cock, the pleasure almost too much for him. His fingers find her pussy, but only to gently play around the outside of it. He watches for her cunt to shoot the necessary signals to her clit to bring it to full bloom, whereupon he has her on her feet, then on his shoulders so that his tongue now does the work his fingers had started. She sits on his neck, not wrapping her legs around him as Gore's hands on her ass keep her in place, his tongue now jetting ever so slightly in and out of her cunt, now flowing a mighty river.

Gore falls onto his back, turns Tamar over so that he can see her ass and cunt, access both with fingers and tongue, and so that she can lean over his stomach and suck on his cock. Her tongue is on his head, inside the foreskin before she pulls the skin from the head again and sinks as much of the cock into her mouth as she can. She manages a comfortable six inches and doesn't try for more, Gore enjoying the work she is doing already, needing no more. Gore is licking her cunt, the entire surface of it, and finding her ass. He sends his tongue into her tight ass with added force, the tight hole needing it. The extra push sends more tongue into her ass than was in her cunt.

Gore is again sitting up, then standing, his hands on Tamar's ass so that she knows she won't fall. Everyone watches as she doesn't skip a beat on his cock, his tongue not losing a centimeter in her ass. They continue on each other's private parts in full public view until Tamar starts a total flood, a salmon-scented stream that Gore laps up like a hungry bear. He then lifts her off his shoulders and cradles her, like a baby, adding to the total sense that no more can ever pass between them. But then Gore is kissing her, moving his lips from hers only for the moment it takes for him to split her legs, her one leg over his shoulder, the other hanging down his chest so that her pussy is exposed to the fingers on the hand that isn't holding her up. He kisses her deep and long without touching her pussy though.

Then a finger is in her curls, on her clit, dancing over her cunt. She holds onto the arm holding onto her as she braces herself for the finger that seems like it might enter her at any minute, any second. Gore's lips on hers provide her with a sense of security however that soon has her hanging comfortably off him, surrendered to what she knows he intends to do. His fingers become more and more insistent, more intentional as her arousal becomes more and more apparent, the moisture signaling what her mouth cannot, trapped sensually in his. Their kisses are long, pauses so brief that they are negligible. The tip of his finger finally makes entry, a finger as thick as any cock in the camp. Tamar's cunt squeezes so tightly over it that he stops short of an inch.

Gore lifts her again so that her pussy is in his face. His tongue is on her clit again, inside her pussy only as deep as his finger had gone. He licks the shit out of her pussy, his tongue pulling another flow from inside her so that her cunt quenches his thirst completely. She jerks under his tongue, his hands keeping her from flying off his shoulders. Again, he brings her towards climax, close enough to start dripping again, to start jerking again. He pauses now so that her pending climax pauses as well, the jerks more rapid during a pause, becoming a rapid shiver. Gore enjoys having her shudder at his touch, un-intimidated by his size, turned on by it.

Gore's tongue in her ass is powerful enough to part her cheeks. He licks the entire surface of her ass, wetting the slit and then biting into the cheeks so that Tamar's pussy starts to drip its own juice, fusing this warm liquid with the moisture from Gore's mouth. Her shivering becomes a continuous constant now, Gore convinced that he has Tamar's body exactly where he needs to have it in order for him to take the intimacy to the next level. Gently, very gently, he sends a thick finger into the tight vagina he's massive cock now craves, but again only one inch is inside Tamar before she starts to wince again. Gore dances around the inch he's been given and watches Tamar closely for any sign that she might be ready for more.

It's his licking of her cunt however, that makes it most fuck ready. He relieves the pussy of his finger and sends his tongue into it again, Tamar completely shivering, the pleasure consuming her completely so that she is momentarily unaware of herself. Gore's tongue re-orientates her as easily as it disorientates her and she is now drifting effortlessly between a million blisses that make location irrelevant. What is clear is that Gore has the entire situation under control. His finger feels the inside of her pussy again, hoping that now he can achieve more than an inch. He does, but just barely. Almost two inches of his finger is inside Tamar's tight pussy before again there is massive internal resistance.

Gore's cock now aches wildly for the inside of Tamar. His finger works her pussy gently until it is a slippery warm cove of two inches. He squeezes his voluminous dick head and touches it to the outside of the cunt. He eases a bit of it onto the surface of the entrance, pushing gently without forcing. He manages the first half of the head, a little over an inch, into the hole. Suddenly his entire head is inside Tamar, whose pussy bites down hard on the large dome that now occupies and effectively blocks the entrance to her vagina. Tamar holds tightly onto Gore's neck, her tiny body square to his as she suddenly jumps up onto his waist and tries to wrap her legs around him while lifting herself away from his cock. His dick's thick tip doesn't release the cunt.

Holding her tightly Gore eases them both to the ground, his massive frame atop her tiny body which now quivers, half fear half anxiety. Very slowly, he pushes down onto Tamar, his cock into her. The squeeze is incredibly tight. Instead of thrusting, the gentle giant nudges his dick into the tight hole, just millimeters achieved on each nudge. Every aspect of Tamar's vagina fights against the entry, making every little gain a massive achievement, the pain of holding himself back from ramming into the hot tight cunt now visible in thick beads of salty sweat raining from Gore. But he will not give her anymore of him than she is able to handle. After what feels like hours, Gore has managed another inch or two in addition to his head.

The crowd is upon them once it becomes clear what they're trying to do. Eyes strain to catch a glimpse of where Gore has stuffed Tamar's tiny cunt. She can't look at him now, her head to the side as she tries to will herself to take this monster into herself. She wants him, with her head, and her heart. But her body is so tightly wrapped that it seems to want to counter his advances. Every time he tries to thrust into her, he manages only a gentle nudge as Tamar's cunt seems to push him out. She eventually looks him in the eyes, drawing him close, and kisses him and then whispers so that only he can hear, "I'm a virgin."

"I'm sorry...I'm so sorry." Gore is suddenly panicked, looking at his cock in the entrance to Tamar's femininity as though he were invading her now and not gently penetrating her.

"No, don't be sorry. I want it to be you. Make me a woman. Please Gore, I want you to make me a woman." Tamar is almost pleading.

Gore gives her a look that speaks what no words ever could. Despite his appreciation of the confidence that she has placed in him, the honor she has presented him with, he suddenly feels the incredible pressure that comes with being handed the responsibility of someone's virginity. Also, given that sex would already be complicated given their proportions, that Tamar is a virgin has just added a remarkable dynamic to this complication. But Tamar's eyes say that she will not move until he has done what she wants. Gore's cock swells at the thought of being the first inside her, all the way inside her. This swelling draws a whimper from Tamar, a frown from Gore, and then a smile from both of them.

Every part of him wants to remove his cock, which is causing Tamar visible discomfort. But to do so would mean that he would have to put her through the process of penetration again. So he stays put, still just nudging, gently, not forcing, moving his broad hips left and right, and then slowly towards the inside of her vagina. He has to concentrate hard on Tamar, making sure that he doesn't hurt her unintentionally. Slowly he etches forward, pushing so completely against her pussy that he drags the walls inward. Gore is the most patient lover despite his brutish demeanor, and after a long while, he is at a panting Tamar's wall. She can't move, needing him to trust himself enough to break through without breaking her.

Tamar squeezes herself around Gore, every part of her against every part of him she can reach. Instinct tells Gore to withdraw his thick meat from inside her, but he reminds himself of the predicament this will leave Tamar in. He pushes against the wall again, gently, and then half an inch back. Again, his thick cock, the domed tip of it, is against the wall, again dragging half an inch towards the exit, and then pushing for the wall again. Gore gets his cock into the first real thrust eventually, no more than an inch away from Tamar's final wall of resistance each time. This causes her walls to sweat volumes of lubrication, coating Gore generously so that his thrusts increase to a two-inch reach. Still he just nudges at the wall.

The thrusts bring Tamar to the doors of another almost orgasm, her millionth one. She can't take it anymore, the look on Gore's face also indicating that he is on the verge of withdrawing and taking himself to the place he's gotten her to. She gives the massive frame an intense squeeze and then pushes herself into him. She lets out a scream, letting Gore know that it's too late; there is nothing that he can do to reverse it, to pull the part of his cock that has broken the delicate flesh that had kept Tamar a girl for so long. But now she was a woman, and his thick cock was now lodged passed the part of her that had resisted him for almost four hours. But now he was in.

Gore doesn't move, contorting himself instead so that he can kiss Tamar. He waits for her to adjust, to respond as appropriately as she needs to before he makes his own response. He mouths a thousand thank you's as she starts to dance her vagina around his cock, which is absolutely throbbing. He gives her a few more minutes and then he is thrusting, pulling his cock out to the entrance, the head staying inside, and then pushing to the furthest reaches of her cunt. Tamar has three orgasms before Gore is even aware of the approach of his own. But soon he is less gentle, Tamar's vagina doing all the right things so that he knows that he can now proceed with fucking her.

There are indications of some discomfort still, but only brief moments of it. She is now wriggling under him as he pounds his massive penis deep and hard into her. She has no response to this and does what feels natural. She grabs him as he pulls another orgasm from her and then falls back as he needs a little distance between them to give his cock more reach. He takes her breasts in hand, then her hips, and then he cups her ass and pulls her to him as he gets incredibly close to shooting his load. She braces herself for his climax, surrendering to him completely, giving up all rights to her body for as long as it will take for him to extract the pleasure from it that he needs.

Tamar manages to come up to him, close enough for a kiss. It's the shortest kiss they've had, Gore suddenly lost in the heat of her vagina. Tamar arches back again, her head almost on the floor, her back a perfect curve. Gore is now positively ramming her tiny cunt, the scene completely reigniting the fuck fest, everyone around them now finding holes and dicks. Her breathing is as heavy as Gore's grunting is loud. He cannot hold himself back now and sends well over half of his massive rod into Tamar so that he knows that he will explode any second.

Gore fucks Tamar so powerfully that she has one final orgasm. Gore shoots torrents of hot liquid into her just as her pussy sprays the drizzle it can manage after so many complete climaxes. Their fluids fuse as Gore lodges deep inside her and Tamar takes an additional four inches. Neither of them moves now, everyone watching shifting their focus to the person they're now also getting closer and closer to climax. Tamar shakes slightly now, Gore jerking in total spasms sporadically. They embrace, Gore's cock inside Tamar going flaccid and getting hard, flaccid and then hard as they start to whisper the possibilities of their lives together in each other's ears.

Near the river, Carmanita is contemplating the water in the midday sun. The four virgin-crazed generals spot her, staying out of sight, watching. Carmanita is in the water eventually, doing her thing, unaware of her audience. For the first time her bathing is about nobody and nothing but herself. The only man in her head now is Razar. She is pleased that the others are having so much fun, and she is convinced now that all she would have to do is ask for the release of the women who want to get back to their husbands and fiancés. She's half-naked in the cool water, enjoying the coolness now that she has accomplished her clean up. After taking a final dip, she swims for the bank where she lays herself out in the delicious sun to dry.

A shadow blocks the sun and she sits up. Carmanita is surrounded by the four men who had brought her before Razar, taunted her in his presence, and made it clear that she was nothing but trouble-causing, disposable cunt. Drawn daggers are all the warning she needs not to make a sound as the men drag her further from the camp, under the shelter and seclusion of the thick willows. Carmanita strains to see if there is even the slightest chance that anybody could have seen her. But it's unlikely now, given the darkness of the canopy under which they now are, her back cold against the muddy floor, the men around her, already undoing their trousers.

Her legs are parted violently, the cold dampness on which she lies immediately sending a shiver up her exposed pussy. She tries to wriggle away from the cold, to lift her ass off the wet, but she is forced back down as the men manage to get their pants down to their knees, exposing lengthy, veiny, solid scepters ready to dig into her immediately. Panic etches on her face as her mouth fails her. She can't speak, she can't breathe, and so she can't scream. She isn't ready for the kind of sex that is about to be forced on her. She isn't even ready for the gentlest lovemaking, she doesn't think. But now, in this dark, damp place, she is about to be raped by four men who have dicks large enough to hurt her even if hurting her wasn't their intention. She knows that it is the express intention of these men to hurt her badly.

Four cocks descend on her face. The tools rub against her delicate skin, on her tightly shut lips, the heads dig into her ears. Then there is cock on her breasts and the soft skin on her stomach. They try of pry her mouth open, Carmanita clenching her teeth shut, refusing to receive the cock now brushing her teeth. Then her legs are being pulled apart, and her pussy tapped. The fingers on her cunt stirring the surface, taunting her with the idea that she is about to have some substantial cock inside her. Carmanita is paralyzed with fear, her cunt shut tight from deep inside, something that will make penetration excruciating.

The hands all over her are rough, hard, and unforgiving. Carmanita's eyes are tightly shut now as she tries to dismiss the situation. She wants to be anywhere but here. Suddenly there are shots of saliva on her cunt, a series of hot wet blobs, which cool quickly. She knows that at any minute her cunt is going to be ripped open by one of these dicks, maybe more than one, her body tightening further at the thought. She accepts the possibility that she might not – cannot – possibly survive this vicious attack. Carmanita tries to will her thoughts to Razar as a finger suddenly pulls on her clit, its tip on the entrance to her virginal pussy.

Suddenly there is silence, the hands on her absent. She cannot open her eyes even as she senses the men around her getting up. There is a gentle hand lifting her before her eyes open and she sees that Razar has appeared out of nowhere and that the generals now have their private parts covered, their erections gone. They disappear sheepishly behind the willows, flanked by ten soldiers that had come with Razar in search of Carmanita. There is no doubt from the look on the soldiers' faces, the look in Razar's eyes, that the four generals will not be alive in a minute. So sooner are the men out of sight, and Razar and Carmanita are in the water, Razar cleaning all evidence of the generals from off of Carmanita. Then he carries her the distance to his tent.

Inside Razar's tent, Carmanita is given a drink, warm, red, and woody. The taste is somewhere between bitter and berries. It warms her immediately. Razar stokes the small fire at the center of his tent, warming the cool space, which doesn't benefit from the sun outside. The room glows a deep orange, and Carmanita is visibly relaxed now despite realizing her nakedness. Razar's cock has been recognizing her nakedness since they entered the tent, his dick again protruding four inches above the top of his trousers. He settles next to her and runs his fingers over her so as to calm her further. She is now warm and relaxed, her attack forgotten and the sight of Razar's manhood arousing her.

Carmanita doesn't feel the need to pretend anymore. She doesn't need to hide her virginity from the man who discovered it all by himself. And since he saved the very same virginity from a savage assault, she feels compelled at the very least to plant her lips on his. Razar holds the kiss as long as he can before his entire body goes into sexually charged overdrive, his cock pulsating at the thought that the lips between her legs conceal as much heat as the lips on her beautiful face. Carmanita pulls Razar so close to her that he falls onto her and she is pushed onto the heap of linens that make up the bed. His weight is comfortable and adds very quickly to her desire to be held by him.

"I won't take you unless you want me to," he says.

There is a softness in his words that makes Carmanita look up at him. She looks it him without defiance, and sees the man behind his cold eyes, a man she can let herself want. Razar sees this, her walls coming down, quickly. The moment is his to take and so he takes it, before he loses the opportunity, or the nerve. His desire for Carmanita is sealed only once she exposes her own desire for him as well. He really needs her to want him before he allows himself to completely want her or believe that he can have her.

His lips fall onto hers warmly again. The new softness of his lips is unexpected and Carmanita kisses him back in an attempt to confirm this tenderness. Over and over he places his lips on hers, taking her upper lip, then her lower lip between his. His mouth tugs on hers gently. The softness of his kisses is never once lost and she finds herself weakening more and more under his control. Razar adjusts her and himself on his makeshift bed. He rises only to take his own clothes off. She watches him undress, her arousal continuing to grow.

The contours of his body are perfect. There are lines where they should be and Carmanita is reminded of the many men she herself shared fantasies about with some of her friends. Watching Razar undress in front of her, she realizes that any distinction between him and any of the other men she had been raised to prepare herself to marry was created for the benefit of keeping her eyes in the fold. She can't even imagine that there is much difference between the cock between Razar's legs and any cock in the gypsy troupe. From what the others had told her about the warriors who'd bedded them, the difference was mostly stylistic.

He gets on top of her, her eyes still on his cock. Razar distracts her by lifting her face towards his and again kissing her on the mouth. He lets his fingers find the middle of her legs and places his palm on her warm pussy. She can't help pushing her cunt against his hand and he smiles

knowing that she has given him permission to touch her. Razar takes a finger, dips it into Carmanita's mouth, and then finds her clit with the wet finger. He makes a slow entry while she holds onto his forearm. He pushes the finger into her opening, her flowering vagina, and the pussy moistens with every stroke.

His finger is inside her, his other hand on her breasts, her lips on hers. Carmanita is literally flowing now in anticipation for Razar, who is as anxious as she is to get inside her. But he knows better, that the illusion of his finger inside her belies the reality of cock inside virgin pussy. So he makes certain that he warms her up adequately, getting her as wet as he can. Her fingers move with all their inexperience over his cock. The sensation makes him drip from the tip. He lets her touch him, enjoying her delicateness. His touches are more certain, he knows what he's doing.

She's on her back, her pussy wet. Razar mounts her and positions his cock on her hole, his lips on her mouth. His kisses are now hot and deeply passionate, his hand on the cock needing to get inside her. He eases his dick forward, a gentle thrust until his dick head is wrapped in the warmth of Carmanita's vagina. She pushes up on him, anxiety overtaking her arousal as the sudden presence of thick cock inside her is realized. She needs to brace herself for the penetration and Razar, aware of this, pauses. Carmanita kisses him long, delaying his cock just long enough for her to adjust to that part of it already inside her.

Razar digs his cock into her slowly. Every time she pushes up on him, he withdraws a little, sending a little more in once she relaxes her push. Slowly but surely progress is made into Carmanita's fiery cunt, the heat beautiful around Razar's solid dick. Deeper into her he goes, her resistances less frequent as she starts to relax into the possibility, the almost certain probability that shortly he will have penetrated her vagina completely. He is in no hurry though, and continues to penetrate her slowly.

Once he reaches the part of her vagina that needs breaking there is a long pause. He takes her face in his hands and forces her to look at him. He checks her eyes for certainty, for confirmation. She is quick to give it, grabbing on to his large forearms tightly when she realizes what her permission means. The pressure in the back of her vagina is intense, as though Razar was trying to push his penis through her and plant it into the soil underneath her. He thrusts gently against the soft tissue, increasing the pressure with each thrust. She kisses him harder that she has since they arrived in the tent and Razar gives a final effective stab through the back of her precious pussy. There is a loud exhalation from both of them as her virginity is broken, Razar breathing into her neck before kissing her there.

The love that passes between them is beautiful. Razar takes full control of Carmanita's vagina once she makes the complete transition from virgin. He moves in and out of her lovingly, as gently as he did before but more fully. His cock reaches all the way back inside her and pulls almost all the way out. The push and pull on the walls of her pussy, walls that wrap fold for fold on Razar's dick, bring every one of Carmanita's fantasies into reality. He makes love to her in one long fluid movement until the day becomes the night, and the night becomes dawn.

"I think I've fallen in love with you," Razar says eventually.

"It would appear then that you have fallen in love with a witch," Carmanita reminds him.

"No, I have simply been bewitched by a woman..." Razar sinks himself into the heat between Carmanita's thighs and fucks her a few more times before he allows her to fall asleep wrapped in his protecting arms.

4 THE BANG CLUB

The rain fell outside but offered absolutely no relief from the sweltering heat. The incessant sound of hornets irritated the small group not so much for the sound, but for the fact that they could not see them. The sound seemed to come from all around the tiny apartment in the cramped backpackers. The cancelled hike into the country was what brought the eight English-speaking tourists into the room of the three Americans in the group. It was decided that they would make up for the lost hike by drinking beer and making fun of each other's countries. The rest of the group was from Britain and South Africa.

The girls were all from South Africa; three students in their twenties had come out to Asia as a gift to themselves for doing well on their final exams. Natalie, Lucinda, and Uchell were beautiful leggy blondes with the telltale tans of a pampered life under the African sun. Luke and Ethan were brothers from North London. In their mid-twenties, they were tall, pale footballers on break from an intense training camp. Jabari, Bakeem, and Nate were three African Americans, college students in the graduate program at MIT. They too were taking a break from hectic college work and were rewarding themselves for a semester well spent. They also played college ball.

The girls sit around in tank tops and tiny shorts, their shoes discarded. The boys all wore board-shorts except for Bakeem, who has a piece of cloth wrapped around his waist, a style he's held on to comfortably since Thailand. The guys were all shirtless. All of them have the physique of pro-athletes. The conversation is academic for the most part, until the beer and the cards come out. A few political jokes follow some serious debate, but this lasts only as long as it takes Jabari and Nate to get back with replenished stocks of beer and a few bottles of tequila.

It isn't long before the game of cards is abandoned for reckless discussions about puberty, first sexual experiences, and current fantasies. The boys seem intrigued by the vivid descriptions the South

Africans give of their fantasies, speaking in tandem as though they are one person having the same fantasy. They speak as if they deliberately want to arouse the five men in the room with them, strewn carelessly on the floor, half on mattresses, half not. Bakeem soon lays on his stomach in an effort to hide his cock, the others adjusting their own dicks in their shorts.

The tequila goes around once more, and then the girls decide that they would further torture the dicks in the room by losing their tank tops and suggesting body shots. This catches the men by surprise as all of them in the room, the girls included, are straight as arrows, upstanding model students who have incredible discipline or else they would not have made the significant achievements they have. But Bangkok is like Vegas: you do crazy things here that you wouldn't dare do anywhere else because Bangkok knows how to keep a secret.

The African Americans are much more adventurous than the Brits, and it isn't long before they're licking salt off bellies, picking up shots out of belly buttons and biting lemon wedges from delicate necks. Most of the licking that follows is more indulgence than necessity, and since the girls aren't complaining, the envelope keeps being pushed a little further. It isn't long before Ethan and Luke get in on the action in true British fashion, pouring tequila up sexy elongated legs and then licking it up all the way to the inner thigh. The other guys see the possibilities of this and dare with all the American arrogance in them to rid the females of their shorts, leaving the super sexy vixens in nothing but bikini bottoms tied by tiny strings at the sides.

Bakeem is the first to let his tongue graze lightly over Natalie's cunt, and when the pussy follows him as he lifts his head to check for resistance, he knows that the game is about to be elevated. It's up to him and Natalie now to give the cue to the others, in the hope that they will take it. The rain pouring down outside sets the perfect atmosphere for the kind of fucking that is possible if everybody lets go and plays nice. Natalie lifts her cunt towards Bakeem, whose head is between her legs. She sways her hips from side to side before settling her ass back on the floor. Bakeem's tongue is already out of his mouth as he follows her down, zones in on the pussy, and gives her bikini several hard licks so as to appease the vagina beneath the fabric.

Suddenly all eyes fall on the two who have just taken body shots to a whole other level. Bakeem keeps his tongue running over the covered cunt as he pulls at the string that releases the fabric from Natalie's hips. He carefully pulls the striped material off her front and exposes the most perfect pussy he's ever seen. A moment is required to simply soak it all in. The perfection of the pink is incredibly inviting.

Now that the cunt is exposed, Bakeem approaches with a little more caution. He licks gently over the vagina, teasing the entrance and then ever so delicately dances his tongue over her clit. She writhes underneath him, encouraging him to be a little more aggressive as the frustration is apparently too much for her. Again though, he delicately circles her pussy with his tongue and then finds the entrance to her Eden where he again gives only the suggestion of penetration and nothing else.

Natalie is not one to take things lying down and she throws her legs around his neck, locking him in place. Everyone applauds her as she makes it clear that playtime is indeed over. Bakeem's lips cover her pussy and then his tongue searches briefly for the entrance. Finding it, he enters her. Again, he is slow and deliberate, frustrating Natalie who squeezes tighter. She achieves the desired result as the hot tongue is suddenly inside her completely. Bakeem breathes through his nose as he tongue-fucks Natalie who has no intention of letting him go anywhere until he's satisfied her.

His powerful tongue washes over the sides of her pussy with the force of any dick. He reaches far inside her and opens her up with wide, wild circles that have her aching to be fucked. She gushes liquid heat from inside her and Bakeem laps it up. The taste of the pussy in his mouth has his dick push so hard against the cloth that it comes undone, leaving his rock-hard cock exposed and the light cloth just hanging loosely over his ass. There is no time for him to worry about exposing himself. It's already too late, as most of his cock has already been seen by everyone in the room.

Natalie grabs hold of his head and holds him in place as he takes her to the last place she thought she'd be when they started playing. The orgasm is so complete that that when she opens her eyes again, it takes her a while to register where she is and even to recognize her friends. When she does, she feels for the bikini, the other girls helping her. Bakeem is left on his knees with ten solid inches of black cock pointing in the direction of the chick whose cunt he just drained. He leaves the group making dinner plans for the next day as he goes to take his dick for a ride in the bathroom.

There is a roar of applause as Bakeem

cums very loudly behind the thin walls. He exits to a hero's welcome. It isn't long before the boys are scheming ways to take all three pussies for a ride. They'll be in the same room eating dinner together tomorrow. It is decided that food won't be the only thing on the menu. Condoms become more important than the balance of the tequila and the boys hit the town, to burn off some steam and also to find a supplier of quality protection.

The girls are caught in their own scheming. They also want to explore the meat that they suddenly have at their disposal. There was always the initial Asian fantasy but that could always be explored later. For now, there are three African Americans and two Brits who need taking care of, and their cunts have been largely deprived of any real action in their overcommitment to their academic pursuits. So they too hit the town, to let their hair down a bit and also to find out where they can get some plucking, waxing, and allover body massaging done the next day so that come dinnertime, they will be good enough to eat.

Bangkok doesn't disappoint either party as they both find what they want. Plans are made and then the night is thoroughly enjoyed. Even though they are offered sex by the locals, the boys decline, saving all their energy for the next day. The girls decline for the same reason. They're also hoping beyond hope that they will not be disappointed because all of a sudden every dick in Bangkok seems to have suddenly spotted them. But this is always the case when it comes to fucking: only once you have made your selection does every other available fuck seem to pick you up on their radar!

The American's room is little changed from the day before, except that this time they've laid all their mattresses on the floor. The girls are the last to arrive and find all the boys in shorts again, vests too this time despite this evening being hotter than yesterday's. Natalie is immediately on Bakeem, taking the ketchup on the side of his mouth onto her tongue and then between her lips. She gives his face a few more licks just to be sure that she's gotten it all and also to make certain that there are no misunderstandings about why everyone has gathered here tonight.

Luke and Ethan are not as shy today and pull Uchell between them on the mattress, offering her a drink and some chow mein all at once. The girls are less interested in the food than they are in the men eating it, but since this is a dinner invite, they eat. Nobody finishes their take-out though, which doesn't offend Jabari who took the liberty of ordering for everyone. He just pours the drinks and lightens the mood further with a few jokes and a remark aimed directly at his cock, warning it that it had better eat all its food tonight.

Lucinda helps Jabari serve the alcohol and then set up the remaining booze in a makeshift bar roughly center of the group, using ice buckets filled with what is now cold water that Nate has negotiated from downstairs. She then finds herself seated between the two of them, her upper body on Nate's and her legs on Jabari's lap. The conversation is easy, flowing effortless between private chatter among the members of each little group and a slightly louder more general conversation that hangs comfortably over the entire room. The alcohol quickly becomes secondary as hormones do in minutes what would have taken the booze slightly longer to achieve.

Bakeem has had his mouth on Natalie's since she arrived, and even now still he kisses her. The men tease him, telling him that he's supposed to fuck her not marry her. Natalie raises her middle finger to the room and uses her other hand to pull Bakeem's down onto her belly, under the hot pants, which give way easily, thanks to the elastic waist, and helps his long middle finger find her cunt. Bakeem sends half his finger into her, Natalie lifting herself slightly and then resting her feet firmly back on the floor. Bakeem stirs the inside of her cunt slowly at first, the passion in her kisses increasing as the stirring in her vagina becomes a twister.

Luke and Ethan remove Uchell's shorts and panties in one go, taking the cue quickly. She's on her back before Ethan finds her mouth, then her breasts, and then settles into her mouth again. Luke is on her manicured cunt, licking first and then sucking on her budding clit before letting two fingers make a measured entry into her tight vagina. Ethan raises his eyes without removing his mouth from hers and glances at Luke's fingers darting in and out of Uchell who has parted her bent legs and kept both feet on the floor so as to anchor herself for what is proving to be an intense assault.

A little ways further Lucinda lies between Nate and Jabari, their shorts off, hers too. She gets up on all fours and faces their feet, her knees between their heads. The two have a view of and access to Lucinda's cunt and ass, and she has access to their cocks as they form a double sixty-nine, Lucinda between them as opposed to on top of just one. She takes Jabari's cock into her mouth first while her hand mimics on Nate's what her tongue is doing to Jabari's. She moves between the two cocks, wetting them equally and then letting her hands work up and down the shafts simultaneously. The two have yet to touch her delicate bits, her handling of their cocks too good a show.

A finger finally finds the inside of her cunt. It's a long powerful tool and pushes into her so firmly that she is jolted forward. Another hand pulls her back, as the finger becomes three and then four in her wet cunt. Her ass is visited by two fingers, which drive into her at an angle that confirms that they belong not to the man whose fingers are in her cunt. She doesn't look back to get her bearings, focusing instead on the pulsating rods, both past the twelve-inch mark, perfectly trimmed at the heads, glistening as she again coats them with the contents of her mouth.

Natalie takes Bakeem into her mouth, which is as hot over his cock as her cunt was over his finger. He takes a long sniff of the finger that still has her scent on it and then watches his chocolate disappear between the perfect strawberry lips belonging to the vanilla pod he knows he's going to pop open later. Her mouth stretches as far as it needs to so that Bakeem's meat moves in and out of her mouth against just enough resistance from her lips to provide his cock with some seriously sensual friction and to keep it from lodging too far back in her throat. They share the duty of maneuvering the man-meat. Now his hands are in her hair, on her head, pushing her onto his meat and him pushing his meat into her mouth. Then it's Natalie, with both hands on the base of the cock, working every one of the elements that make up her mouth over every part of Bakeem's dick that will fit inside it in what Bakeem's dick, could it speak, would describe as an oral orchestra playing out a symphony on his cock.

If this were a competition, though, then Uchell would have won the jackpot. Luke has the biggest dick in the room. Of course she knows that there will be some sharing going on, but with the almost fifteen inches of thick English dick, there is no doubt that there is more than enough to go around. Ethan's cock is not as impressive, but for a man of his height, a few inches short of six feet, his ten inches are relatively excessive. Uchell takes Luke's boa in her mouth, just the massive head, and uses her hands to milk the length of the tool, staring up at him in anticipation of a drink. Ethan places his own cock between her thighs and rubs his cock against her clit.

Everyone settles into the established positioning of dicks and fingers, mouths and cunts, and the room is suddenly silent except for the heavy breathing and almost subdued moaning. Each person, each little group despite being absolutely overwhelmed by the pleasure being given them, has the sense almost that they are in a room filled with sleeping babies that they don't want to wake up. Nothing changes for a while, the situation perfect. Everyone has found everyone else's spot, and they work those spots until it seems they might end the carnival too soon. The girls will not have it and decide to turn the carnival into a full on parade. They release themselves from their respective cocks almost simultaneously.

The boys don't take much coaxing to line their cocks up once the girls have decided and made it clear to them that this is the best way for them to get a sample of every cock in the buffet. All their shorts are off and the few tops still on find the floor. The three women walk up and down the dick lineup, feeling every rod, stroking and tugging at the tools ready for war. Natalie closes her thighs over Luke's dick, a large part of it protruding on the other side, below her butt. She squeezes tightly and he starts to thrust. Lucinda's mouth meets his cock on the other side and she takes as much as she can into her mouth, Luke still thrusting even once Natalie has dismounted and left Lucinda to handle the mammoth task on her own.

Natalie makes her way to Ethan, Bakeem not looking too impressed. Ethan immediately pushes her to her knees and points his cock in the direction of her open mouth. Natalie gives a taunting look at Bakeem as she takes Ethan's vanilla rod into her mouth. Bakeem watches Ethan fuck her perfect mouth, his cock going deep into the mouth his dick had just occupied, and then fucking her throat in short jabs before making a partial exit, wet and warm, and then shooting back into her. Natalie holds on to Ethan at the knees, his hands on her head as he moves his cock around in her mouth and her mouth around on his cock.

Luke's cock finds the inside of Natalie's ambitious mouth next, Bakeem having pulled Lucinda down on his own meat. Bakeem wants to return the favor by taunting Natalie with his expert handling of Lucinda. Luke wants to challenge the overconfident Natalie, who teased his cock between her thighs with the arrogance of a woman whose cunt had seen and felt better. England had invaded South Africa before, a lesson that Natalie seemed to have forgotten. Luke was more than prepared to remind her of it. Regardless of their intentions with each other though, fun was about to be had by all.

Lucinda is the one who has Bakeem on

his knees. She is on his shoulders, half-sitting even though her feet are firmly on the ground. Bakeem's mouth is where we would see her cunt if it wasn't already completely swallowed by him. Her hands block his ears as his tongue tells her vagina things that nobody else in the room is supposed to hear. Bakeem's fitness is incredible, his upper body strength phenomenal. He moves his torso up and down, carrying Lucinda on the muscles of his neck at times, as he eats out her pussy with no support from his hands. He has the ability to keep her up, along with himself, without losing the rhythm of his cunt crunching. Natalie's eyes fall on this display just as Luke sends more of his cock than she anticipates into her mouth.

If it were slightly more solid, the enormous cock in her mouth might have done some significant damage. But Luke's cock is thick, heavy, but not hard. It is every bit like a snake, a python, or a boa, weighty, powerful, but able to writhe and coil, and bend and curve as needed. She lets the serpent fill her mouth and then sink its head down her throat. Luke shoots his tool into her repeatedly, each thrust pulling her from her distracted gaze in Bakeem's direction, Lucida now hanging over Bakeem's shoulders so that his cock is in her mouth and his mouth is still completely possessed of her pussy.

Tired of the game that Natalie and Bakeem have made so obvious Luke releases her from dick duty and makes his way to where Uchell has Nate screaming like a little girl. There is no room for inhibition, no place for unfounded concern for sleeping babies as Uchell takes the entire length of Nate's perfect penis into her mouth. It's impossible, from a biological point of view. But they all see it, every inch of Nate's solid dick completely enveloped by Uchell's mouth. The display raises the value of Uchell's mouth significantly, as it becomes prime real estate, the most desired location for every cock wishing to relocate. Nate makes Luke wait before finally allowing him a private viewing of this property.

Uchell is anything but overwhelmed. She covers her pearly whites with her lips and chews her way slowly down the lengthy muscle. Luke braces himself for what his eyes tell his head will be bites, but his cock soon puts that lie to bed. His dick disappears deeper and deeper into Uchell, drawing attention from the others who are now suddenly doing nothing but watching. The girls' mouths open wider as more of Luke is swallowed. The guys own cocks go harder as they suddenly realize that the mouth to get to is Uchell's. Luke takes firm hold of her head and slowly thrusts the last bits of his serpent into

Uchell, helping her along with her endeavor. Applause breaks out along with a chorus of wolf-whistles as Uchell's lips make contact with Luke's body, her upper lip in his pubes, and her lower lip on the top of his nut-sack. He gives a few circular thrusts and then slowly, very slowly for the benefit of the others who have now surrounded them, releases his dick, pulling himself reluctantly from its warm perch so as to confirm to all exactly what has just been achieved.

Bakeem is the first to move Luke out of the way. He bends down to plant a long kiss on Uchell's lips before sliding his middle and index into her mouth, as if to confirm that her mouth didn't open into a gaping void at the back. He throws a look at the others that says this chick's for real! His cock replaces the fingers, slowly despite everyone's knowledge of what is possible. But the theatrics of it, the sheer spectacle of cock disappearing into Uchell's mouth demanded this approach. Bakeem also knows that the faster his insertion, the smaller his cock will seem. So he lets his pace extend his dick, an illusion that works mostly in his head. He has nothing to worry about though, none of the men do, their cocks impressive by all accounts. Luke just has an unusually large member, luck of the draw, that's all.

Nate pulls Lucinda onto his cock as

Bakeem's gets the royal treatment. The benefit for the men with less meat is that their dicks are hard, all the way through, and remain so for the duration of their oral treatments, unlike Luke's which doesn't need to get hard, but when it does, stays so for brief intervals, unless he has found the inside of a cunt. Nate and Bakeem send their cocks into the respective mouths, only Bakeem's making a complete entry and then extract almost completely. The show isn't as enticing as Luke's was and so everyone finds a body again. Natalie finds herself surrounded by the remaining men who take turns fucking her mouth, licking her clit, and sending fingers into her slippery vagina.

When Jabari makes his way to Uchell, he finds that he has a little bit of an extended wait, Bakeem very possessive of the mouth. Natalie and Lucinda keep his almost perfectly shaped penis occupied in the interim. Uchell pulls herself from Bakeem eventually, not wanting to be accused of being selective. Also, Jabari's penis is the kind that can almost be described as pretty, and so secretly Uchell has been keenly anticipating this cock in her mouth. The other girls aren't giving way though, and so Jabari soon finds his meat triple-licked and what feels like quadruple-sucked—three tongues, three mouths working on his shaft. Lucinda and

Natalie ambitiously try for all the meat inside them, only Uchell succeeds. Jabari isn't complaining, although he does feel a little robbed of the exclusivity the others enjoyed from Uchell.

Luke pulls Uchell aside again, his cock significantly harder. She positions herself so that his cock falls easily into her mouth. Slowly he starts to insert it, and slowly Uchell makes for the floor in a backward arch. Luke follows, helping her straighten her legs once her back touches the ground and then almost laying over her face so that his hard meat can fuck her mouth. He props himself up with his hands and she places hers near his hips just in case. He sends his dick into her, not all the way, letting her come up for more if she wants it. Each time she rises, taking more into her mouth, he thrusts into her so as to claim the territory gained. Again Uchell manages most of his cock, Luke screaming "fuck me, woman!" so loudly that the others look to see if that isn't exactly what is happening. Luke fucks Uchell's mouth for as long as the position is comfortable for her and then removes his cock, again with the gaping audience in mind.

Ethan lifts Uchell off the floor and onto her knees again. She takes his cock in hand before she's even steady on her knees, and Ethan sends it straight to the back of her mouth. She takes his entire length all in one go and then sucks hard on the meat in her mouth. Her fingers find his balls, and she tugs hard on the sack as Ethan fucks her mouth as though he was five seconds from cumming. He fucks her mouth at the same quick pace for almost fifteen minutes. His last few thrusts slow down, and then he pulls his cock from Uchell, offering her his hot sack, which she swallows completely, swirling the balls around in her mouth and tickling them with her tongue. Ethan pulls on his shaft at the same time with the same quick pace, keeping his orgasm at bay by alternating his hands every few strokes.

Nate replaces Ethan's balls in Uchell's mouth again. Uchell closes her eyes as the dark cock slides down her throat. She purses her lips and then pouts over the meat, but lets Nate fuck her this time with no help. Her head locked in his hands she simply relaxes the back of her throat so that he can shoot his entire shaft all the way in and out of her without choking her. Nate's strokes are not Ethan's. He makes love to Uchell's mouth with long deep lingering strokes, sending her into a lull that has her neck drop back occasionally. Nate catches her each time, steadying her, and then continuing his gentle ravishing of her oral cavity. Uchell joins in after what feels like a million strokes and sucks on the cock as gently as it fucks her throat.

Natalie and Ethan find the floor, each other's genitalia in the other's mouth. Ethan is almost vicious in his mouth fucking. Hard thrusts send his dick so deep into Natalie's mouth that she eventually just leaves it wide open so that his cock can lodge in her throat once and for all. Ethan chews on her cunt with the same vice. She brings her legs up, bending them so that her knees are above his shoulders, and then she squeezes her thighs over his head. Locked in place, he sends his tongue into her, getting inside her with every available inch of his thick tool, lapping up the coating on the inside of her pussy like a kitty cat on warm milk.

Lucinda's cunt is the focus for Bakeem, Luke, and Jabari. All three men have one hand on their own dicks as they send the fingers of the other hand into her pussy. They kneel around her on the floor so that her hands can reach their balls easily. Alternately, the three dip their sacks into her mouth, none of them offering her cock, keeping their dick beating to themselves. Lucinda enjoys the warm nuts in her mouth; she likes the feel of the delicate sacks as they dip, linger, and then lift out of her. Her tongue reaches occasionally for the lifting sack, and sometimes she bites on the pouch closest to her. Bakeem, Luke, and Jabari are all on a steady collision course with climax.

Uchell lets her hand rest on Jabari's dick handling fingers almost as soon as Nate has withdrawn. Nate joins Ethan as they take Natalie's cunt on a roller coaster ride with their fingers. Jabari is hesitant at first but then lets his cock go, surrendering it to Uchell's fingers, her feather-light touch. He turns towards her and then leans so that she can lie down without losing her grip. She strokes his cock, knowing that he wants her to put it in her mouth. Instead, she lets her tongue find his hot sack, and gently she takes the balls into her mouth and chews softly on them. The tip of Jabari's cock starts to drizzle cum.

Bakeem finally has four fingers in Lucinda so that there is no place for anybody else's. He pulls every drop of her arousal to the external surfaces of her cunt in what appears to be an orgasm but really isn't. Lucinda's wet pussy simply drips in gallons as he brings her as close to climax without actually giving her an orgasm. The other men just watch, pulling hard on their cocks and balls, also keeping their own orgasms at bay. Everyone in the room has reached an almost climax when they realize that finally Jabari seems to have exclusive reach and access to Uchell's mouth.

Jabari watches his cock move in and out of Uchell's mouth, his hands on his own head. Uchell's lips dance around the ebony cock, and her lips mask the meat in perfect slivers of pink as she swallows it entirely in her signature style. Everyone in the room is suddenly on their own as they handle their own cunts and their own cocks, watching Uchell and Jabari the whole time. Uchell has brought the entire orgasmic fabric in the room together, and as she weaves her magic on Jabari, she brings everyone towards their own individual climaxes.

There is a huge sigh as the entire situation progresses from mass masturbation to a collective climax. Uchell and Jabari are completely unaware of their own contribution to the orgasms surrounding them, as their own genitals become the epicenters of every fucking sensation they have ever experienced. Uchell spills the contents of her cunt as Jabari dresses her mouth in the contents of his rod. They drink from each other thirstily and yet there is no haste. They take all the time necessary for them to leave each other with no need of additional cleaning. The wait was worth it, not just for Jabari, but also for Uchell.

No invitations are sent out the next day,

but everyone makes a generally steady progression to the American base that has become the official fucking headquarters. Uchell is the only one missing from the group, not entirely unexpected since her jaw took the most strain the day before. Lucinda and Natalie are just excited for the opportunity to regain some of their street cred with the boys. There are no illusions of dinner, everyone simply nibbling on whatever is available from the vending machine at the end of the hall.

Lucinda and Natalie allow themselves to be undressed, the exercise turning the boys on. Nate, Jabari, Bakeem, Luke, and Ethan let themselves move equally over the two sexy vixens, nobody, not even Bakeem, claiming exclusivity. Hands move over breasts, bellies, and cunts; over asses; and up and down thighs as they work quickly to remove clothes. No sooner is everyone naked then are the girls laid out on the mattresses, legs parted before all the cocks except Luke's are dressed in neon-colored plastic sheathes. The boys seem uninterested in the mouths of the two women on their backs. They seem cunt-focused, driven by the promise of the pussy before them. One thing is quickly clear: tonight will be about fucking.

The dismissal of their mouths bothers the two girls momentarily, but soon gives way to the relief that they will not need to compete with the oral ability of the absent Uchell. If it's their cunts that the boys want, then they will focus on making it the best pussy the five have ever had, and hopefully it will be good enough to dethrone Uchell's mouth, which still wears a crown confirmed by the obvious disinterest in their own oral cavities. Thoughts of Uchell's mouth start to fade fast though as tongues make contact with clits and the boys start to prepare the pussies for some significant pounding.

Bakeem lets his cock slip into Lucinda just as soon as the men have all let their tongues dip into the pair of pussies in the room. His cock lowers into her completely and he immediately starts to thrust, full force, creating the room required in the tight hole for his cock to move. It isn't long before his cock moves freely through Lucinda's vagina, but not too freely that it doesn't appreciate the tightness of the wrap. His thrusts are almost as audible as the grunts from his gaping mouth as he relishes Lucinda in her vaginal entirety.

Nate finds Natalie first. He's nestled inside her while Bakeem remains distracted by Lucinda and the others stroke their dicks to maintain solid erections in preparation for their turns. Inside Natalie Nate's cock is caught in the anticipated erotic web that is the inside of her cunt. Her vagina has what feels like a million tentacles, each one dancing across Nate's cock while sucking hard on the solid surface. Inside the warmth there is no room to figure out what part of the sensation is real and which part is simply imagination fueled by anticipation, so he foregoes brain activity for the sake of active fucking.

Lucinda has her chocolate dipstick replaced by Ethan's vanilla once Bakeem manages to pull his cock from her. Ethan takes full advantage of the slippery cunt created, thanks to Bakeem, sending his ten inches in and out of Lucinda with the force sufficient to draw loud panting from her. Everybody looks in her direction as Ethan's overenthusiastic fucking has Lucinda yelping with each stroke. She grabs onto his ass and pushes him deep into her, enjoying the fullness of his thick cock inside her.

Natalie is the first to have her pussy attacked by supersized Luke. Luke was as apprehensive about the choice as was every cunt in the room. Eventually though, it just boils down to the fact that Natalie's is the first available cunt just as Luke takes on his first semi-full erection of the night. He lets his head sink slowly into the slippery hole that is availing itself for him, and Natalie pushes her pussy up so that Luke's dick makes a steady entry into her. The thick dick struggles almost as soon as three inches make entry, however. Natalie determines not to be a problem for the loaded Luke though and forces five more inches into her by raising her crotch to Luke's cock with significant force. Luke forces no more into her and thrusts in and out of her with the eight inches she is obviously comfortable with. Despite the lack of protection, there is no apprehension, Luke unlikely to stay inside her long enough to shoot.

Jabari takes Ethan's place inside Lucinda while kissing her lips softly. This is the first time Lucinda is kissed and this almost surprises her. She finds that her focus is suddenly more on Jabari's lips than on the perfect cylinder that he is driving in and out of her. After all, this was a fuck-fest, but Jabari, in the absolute perfection of his cock, feels the need to kiss passionately the owner of the pussy he happens to be penetrating. Lucinda allows herself the pleasure of this faux lovemaking, and Jabari takes her mouth and pussy on the perfect pleasure cruise.

Luke's cock inside Natalie has no more effect than completely stretching her cunt. She tries for more but is unable to make the concessions that Luke's dick requires in order for it to make a decent go of her pussy. It isn't long before she allows the mammoth serpent to leave her, and she rolls over in Jabari's direction. Lucinda notices that his lips have left her mouth before she realizes that his cock is no longer inside her. The look Natalie gives her immediately placates her irritation, and Lucinda allows her friend to replace her under the gentle Jabari, who positions himself on Natalie just as he had positioned himself on Lucinda, entering her stretched cunt only after he has said hello to her lips. Natalie's vagina very quickly adjusts to the new cock and Jabari gets into a steady rhythm, fucking Natalie with signature perfection.

Luke allows the somewhat smaller Lucinda to slither underneath him, expecting nothing more than contact between cock and flesh. His thick meat had made entry into the more experienced Natalie, but nothing more was achieved. It occurs to him briefly that Lucinda might be possessed of a cunt that went to the same school as Uchell's mouth, but he doesn't let himself dwell too much on this thought. It just seems unfeasible. Lucinda on the other hand, doesn't think too much, simply taking Luke's dick in her tiny hands, guiding it into her cunt and then pulling him down onto himself. She lets out what can only be described as a shriek as every inch of Luke immediately fills her cunt and pins her to the floor. The scream distracts everyone but Luke, whose cock is pulled into the cunt by its owner, and so he knows that she wants whatever it is that his dick is doing inside her.

Nate is quickly on the scene, pushing both Luke and Lucinda so that they are on their side and he is behind her, sending dick into her ass while watching Luke's assault on her cunt. Lucinda has two massive cocks inside her, and suddenly her composure is that of a virgin in a lily pond. She holds herself up on Luke's neck and then relaxes into the ramming from the back and the front. Her mouth purses as she lets out steady breaths, the men fucking her with the precision of experienced soldiers. Nate is the louder warrior, the tight ass hot and fucktastic. Luke is silent, disbelieving as his cock moves in and out of Lucinda as though hers is the cunt for which it was designed.

Ethan's meat is inside Natalie, who remembers her unspoken competition with Lucinda as she takes the Brit into herself and starts to take his cock for a very scenic ride. Bakeem throws her a few looks but takes a deep breath and lets Ethan have his turn. He uses his strength to pull her and Ethan on top of himself and settles his dick in her ass and his lips up and down her neck and back. Ethan fucks Natalie hard, hard enough for the impact to be felt by Bakeem's cock, and so he does nothing but hold the two up on his cock as Ethan does what he needs to do inside Natalie.

Ethan jumps off Natalie with not a second to spare. He's almost shot his load. With the quick extraction, he turns immediately away from the scene and puts his hand on his head, watching as his dick recedes from the finish line, only a few trickles of seed escaping into the condom. It's too soon to cum. Jabari takes his place in Natalie, much to her relief, and Bakeem's. The position Bakeem finds himself in is such that the added weight of another person means that there is significantly more pressure around his cock. Jabari also has what can only be described as nigger swag when it comes to fucking, and so the complete stirring he starts inside Natalie sends a million interesting messages to his cock, messages that Bakeem's dick responds to by getting incredibly thicker, longer, harder, and closer to exploding.

As soon as he gets too close though, his powerful lift sees Natalie off his cock despite the fact that Jabari has just delivered a massive inward thrust, down and hard. He checks out the action on Lucinda and of the two men fucking her, Luke is the one generous enough to avail her cunt to Bakeem. It's actually because he too is so close to cumming that he needs his cock to take a breather in the open air. Nate has no intention of leaving her ass, his own climax still a ways off. Bakeem takes his time entering Lucinda, for the same reasons he took his time filling Uchell's mouth. Lucinda lets him enjoy the moment, needing the depths of her pussy to close over the thinner dick as it enters—fortunately, for her cunt though Bakeem's cock is only thinner by comparison to Luke's, but still thick and imposing by all accounts. Her cunt is soon caught in a chocolate/strawberry/vanilla war that has her pussy pissing sorbet.

With her cunt dripping Lucinda soon finds herself under Luke again, her ass vacant. The other men flock to Natalie and her ass, mouth, hands, and cunt are soon all occupied in an attempt to get her cunt wet and draw her climax outside of her pussy. Luke sends himself all the way into Lucinda and doesn't for a second settle. The complete erection he achieves is a rare treat that he knows will only last as long as he remains in contact with the inside of a vagina. So he keeps send the enormous monstrosity deep into her soon after he has lifted it from her partially.

Lucinda's pussy doesn't need to do any work as every part of it is attended to by Luke's dick. His cock reaches deep inside it and all around, and Lucinda finds that as the cock drags against her walls her climax starts to exit with each stroke, largely without her permission. The fluid secreted by her cunt coats the mammoth cock pulling it from inside her, and Luke is able to make a considerably larger impression on the inner surfaces of Lucinda than he could have hoped for. It isn't long before every part of her cunt is spitting streams of her climax against Luke's cock and spilling this fluid excessively through the very small spaces left for the surplus to escape.

The final stages of her orgasm are beautiful. Luke can only watch as Lucinda is no longer able to move, his cock stationary inside her but pulsating so loudly, throbbing inside her so that it feels like he is still fucking her despite the fact that they have both stopped moving completely. Luke keeps his cock inside Lucinda until she has completely succumbed and been totally drained. There is no juice left inside her cunt when Luke makes his exit, slowly. She cups her cunt affectionately, blocking the entry so that the men who had designs on her pussy know that her vagina is closed for business for the rest of the night. She couldn't take another cock if she wanted to. Even through the fucking fantastic orgasm, she knows that her pussy can take no more, not now, not until it has recovered at least a little bit.

The competitive Natalie cannot help pulling Luke to herself, despite the other men having been so occupied with priming her for their own cocks. But they let the lady have what she wants, more so because it is obvious by the look on Lucinda's face that Natalie will be left wanting even if all of their cocks were shoved into her at once. Luke lets her ease his meat into her cunt herself, and after considerable effort and some obvious discomfort on her part, only the eight or so inches from earlier is inside Natalie. She can do nothing but concede that there just isn't enough cunt for Luke's cock.

It takes Luke a minute to adjust to the restrictive cunt belonging to Natalie, but then he starts to make slow thrusts, deliberately trying not to push any deeper into her than he's already managed. He lifts himself up enough so that he can feel on his entry into Natalie that more of him is being accommodated, but the knowledge of the facts leaves both him and his cock wanting. Luke's dick inside Natalie however has all the effect on her cunt that it had on Lucinda's, and it isn't long before her pussy starts flowing from deep within itself.

Natalie starts to erupt. Despite the increased slipperiness, Luke sticks to his eight-inch penetration. Natalie has no idea just how little cock is inside her in relation to what could be, her cunt consumed by the length and girth she has managed. Her climax is louder than Lucinda's. Strange for Luke since he knows, as does everyone else, that his cock is not inside her completely. He lets himself forget the scene and keeps a steady stroke and rhythm as Natalie's climax comes to a very audible end. Everyone in the room is fixed on Natalie as she slumps down, and Lucinda makes her way next to her as Luke exits. The girls both have their hands on their cunts as the boys surround them, on their knees, removing condoms and stroking their cocks over the bitches reclining on their backs.

As the men get closer and closer, pulling harder and harder on their throbbing cocks, the girls start digging into their cunts. They try for a climax even though the thought seems impossible given the thorough fucking they received from Luke. Closer and closer the boys get, and ever closer the girls get as they make deeper digs into their cunts, their fingers slipping as their pussies get wetter and wetter. The girls climax quicker than they expected, and the boys are super edged on by the show playing out. They start to shoot, making sure to point their cocks over the girls so that they spray their loads over the sensual surfaces shivering with orgasmic pleasure. The girls writhe as the boys redefine body shots and spray every last drop of their load over them.

The next day there is very little conversation. Everyone is in their respective rooms just processing. It's been a fantastic couple of days, the rain nothing but background to their fucking. Uchell has enjoyed her rest and disappears into the streets of Bangkok alone as the girls rest up. The brief tales of the night before have her needing the distraction of the city, hers being the only untouched cunt in the group now. Uchell assumes that Natalie and Lucinda will sleep all day, and so she has no plans to return until evening, which means she'll spend the rainy day in the mall, watching films at the theater and eating local food in the large food court. Nate, Ethan, and Jabari have the same idea, for no other reason other than the fact that their respective roommates have disappeared. But how the boys have occupied themselves is unknown to Uchell, who is well rested and has already forgotten the plight of her neglected pussy.

That Natalie, Luke, Bakeem, and Lucinda have formed a strategic fuck alliance is undeniable. It's barely noon when they've met in the Brit's room, unconcerned for the other four people they've been intimate with over the last while. Immediately they touch each other, not concerned with who touches who really just as long as the four of them are together and are building up towards a pleasant afternoon of fucking. Bakeem and Natalie of course are the closest thing to a couple already so they keep close to one another. Luke and Lucinda are together for no reason other than physiology. Lucinda's cunt is able to take the entire monstrosity that is Luke's cock, and so Luke needs at least one more exclusive exploration of her before he needs to search for another cunt as accommodating.

Luke moves his hands over Lucinda in a manner that can only be described as precise. His hands can wrap almost completely around her legs as he moves both hands up and down the length of her exceptionally long legs, he himself on his knees between them. Lucinda knows she is in expert hands and feels like she is being prepped for an exotic massage. At her thighs, his thumbs dig in and make perfect circles towards the inside of the firm muscle. Lucinda can't help parting her legs, her lips parting as Luke leans in and starts kissing her. She kisses him back easily. Their tongues dance in each other's mouths as their hands dance over each other's bodies.

Natalie's body is far from neglected. Bakeem's hands are as expert, as precise, as Luke's. The only difference is that Bakeem's are not as conservative. He kisses Natalie while immediately finding her cunt with his longest finger. He sends his finger into her as though to remind her that he has first dibs on her cunt and also to guide her memory away from its etchings of Luke and his ridiculously large cock. With his finger locked in place, his other hand travels the measure of Natalie, while his mouth and hers have a deep intimate conversation.

Lucinda immediately starts towards taking on Luke's cock. He releases her as she makes her intention known and then slowly works her way down to his meat. Luke is on his back, Lucinda taking the cock in hand and guiding it towards herself. Both men have their dicks sucked with the same skill with which they had touched the girls. They are not even completely settled into the oral assaults when the girls have already started to draw liquid from their cocks. Both dicks, rock hard, coat the mouths of Natalie and Lucinda as they slide the hot cavities up and down the shafts. Lucinda is not Uchell, but with her cunt, she doesn't have to be. Natalie completely swallows

Bakeem.

Again, Bakeem's fingers are inside Natalie. He pulls her ass closer to him so that he can drive his appendages in and out of her without pulling her too far from his cock for her not to be able to take it into her mouth completely. Her mouth opens wider as three of his fingers slide in and out of her wet cunt, each gasp sending her all the way down on his cock, her mouth closing at the base and then working up the shaft, and the tongue and the lips tight against the throb.

Lucinda is positioned on Luke's cock so that her ass is basically adjacent to Natalie's. This puts her pussy within reach of Bakeem's fingers. He can't help sending one, then two into Lucinda. Her legs part slightly, not moving off her knees though, and he adds a third finger. Three fingers each on both hands are moving steadily in and out of the slippery cunts almost in his face. The girls don't skip a beat on the dicks in their mouths, while Bakeem keeps their cunts flowing in an almost continuous stream. Luke enjoys the enthusiasm of Lucinda's mouth brought about by the ebony fingers in her cunt.

Bakeem's cock is throbbing, extending to maximum length as his ego processes the fact that his fingers are in full possession of all the pussy in the room. This spectacle, while not totally visible to

Luke, sends enough blood to his cock to have it at full mast as well. Lucinda manages to attend sufficiently to the first few inches of the meat with her mouth, her hands on the rest with the force that comes from her bracing herself on the meat, using Luke's power-tool to keep herself up. Bakeem continues his fiery fingering of both of them as Luke makes the slight adjustment required for him to watch Bakeem's assault on both pussies.

Luke suddenly finds that his cock has two tongues moving up the side of the shaft almost fifteen inches long. In fact, it could be longer but suddenly that is irrelevant. The girls play along the length with their tongues and quickly progress to ambitious sucking. Natalie is on his balls when Lucinda is on his head, and then they swap. There are always fingers on the parts of the cock that doesn't have lips or tongue, sometimes teeth on it. Luke closes his eyes as the two take full control of his cock. Bakeem is satisfied with their cunts.

The girls give Luke's cock a good run, but then return to the two-mouth two-cock suck. Both men sucked again, it is still Bakeem with totally pussy monopoly. Luke knows that he doesn't need the distraction. He can't risk losing any of the erection he's achieved. Bakeem gives the cunts a few more solid stabs, working up to four fingers so that it is his hands that prop the girls up from the inside of their cunts. The mouths on their cocks take a few deep sucks, hard enough to indicate to the men that they might be about to lose the hot wrappers on their cocks. This is exactly what happens!

Bakeem doesn't like the removal of his fingers from the girls as they shuffle and swop cocks. It's a brief exit but he can't wait to get his fingers back inside the warm pussies. The girls can't either, they just don't say it. With alternate mouths on alternate cocks, the men are soon sucked into a rhythm that has erections completely restored; Bakeem's fingering is the visual motivation for massive erections. The mouths move over their cocks almost gracefully, a sort of dance as the beginnings of an orgasm start in the depths of the pussies. The men have started to drip themselves.

The girls make it loud and clear that they are in the throws of an orgasm. Luke pulls Lucinda towards him so that her cunt is relieved of Bakeem's fingers. He knows that he needs to take advantage of the condition of her cunt and the solid erection he has reached. Lucinda is on her back almost instantly, Luke inside her immediately. Lucinda is thrusting, pulling Luke into herself at the same time as she tries hard not to lose the orgasm she's started. But the cock inside her is too much for her to dare ride it to a quick climax. She resigns herself to the floor and lets Luke dig his cock into her completely as he then starts, for the first time, to completely fuck her without her assistance.

It doesn't take much for Bakeem to make total entry into Natalie, and he's already made several deep thrusts long before Luke has made his first. His thick dark meat is inside Natalie and making a dance floor for her cunt before Natalie has even decided on her own strategy for the dick. It turns out that no strategy is required as Bakeem takes full fuck control of the tight pussy he's invaded. Natalie is nowhere near voicing any objections as immediately her pussy gives the rod inside her a positive reception.

Bakeem and Luke have little else on their minds but the pleasure of the women underneath them. The women feel the same way but are so consumed by the pleasure being delivered that they can do nothing but receive the dicks dipping into them repeatedly. Bakeem manages to get Natalie on her stomach without removing his cock from her heated cunt. She crawls away from him a bit, as he sends aggressive stabs into her to regain his cock's footing. Her crawling sends her in the direction of Luke's nuts as he absolutely destroys Lucinda's cunt with high exits and way-too-fucking-deep entries. She manages Luke's large nuts in her mouth as she grabs onto Lucinda's legs and parts them further, giving Bakeem a complete view of the most erotic scene so far. His fucking gets as hard as his cock and his intentions as he suddenly realizes the situation he and Luke have managed.

Luke lifts himself completely out of Lucinda as soon as the sensation that is Natalie's mouth on his balls registers. Lucinda doesn't say it, but appreciates the break. She fingers herself, Luke's balls in Natalie's mouth, and Bakeem's own balls over her head. She lifts herself so that the dark orbs find the inside of her mouth, and soon Natalie and Lucinda are sucking on the balls of the cocks that were fucking each other's pussies. Luke can't keep his cock out of Lucinda for long though and pulls his sack from between Natalie's teeth as he sends his dick into Lucinda. He rolls on his side at Bakeem's request, which sends his cock into her ass. It takes some effort, Lucinda's ass not as accommodating as her cunt. It isn't too long though before both men are fucking Lucinda sideways, literally!

The scene has Natalie fingering herself intently. She doesn't have to for long though as Bakeem pulls her to him so that both his and Luke's mouths have access to her cunt just above Lucinda's head and all twenty fingers are also able to make the acquaintance of her pussy. Surprisingly it's Lucinda's fingers that find her cunt first, and she works her friend's vagina so effectively that Natalie is soon dripping onto her face. The boys immediately lap this up, Luke pulling out of Lucinda quickly, quickly pulling Natalie down and on her side so that the girls are facing one another. He sends his cock into her cunt from the back, and in this new position manages twelve complete inches. The girls kiss each other as the boys fuck ass and cunt, respectively. Natalie's pussy is suddenly very warm, very wet, and exceptionally welcoming. Luke takes full advantage.

It takes some coaxing on Natalie's part but Bakeem finally leaves Lucinda's ass. He helps Luke with the adjustment so that his cock doesn't leave Natalie's cunt after he has lodged thirteen inches inside it. They move in unison until she is on top of Luke, her hands on his chest as his cock moves around inside her. Bakeem eases her down so that she can only kiss Luke, her hands aside his neck. He then sends the entirety of his dick into her ass and very quickly sets the pace with incredibly insistent fucking. Luke takes the cue and his too-large-for-this cock starts to fuck her cunt as hard as Bakeem is doing in her ass. Lucinda perches herself over Luke's face to help her friend somewhat and soon finds her own ass and pussy licked by both Luke and Natalie.

Bakeem is soon demanding pussy, trying once he has exited Natalie's ass to send his cock into her cunt along with Luke's. There is no fucking way that this is going to be possible. Luke is so impressed with the inroads that he is reluctant to give up the pussy, offering Lucinda's instead. But Bakeem insists, and so Luke, reminding himself of Lucinda's cunt by shooting four fingers into it, lifts Natalie off his cock. He then drops her onto Bakeem's dick, sliding himself up so that Lucinda can settle herself on his dick before it loses its straight penetrating power. Lucinda is on his cock and has it inside her in seconds. Both girl's ride their respective cocks as the boys relax on the floor and enjoy the view.

There is no way for Luke to resist turning Lucinda over. She wraps her legs around him as they both roll until she is on her back, and he is weighted down on her, his cock so deep inside her that for the first time she is not totally at ease. Luke has the most complete erection he's had since they met the girls, and now his cock drags on the sides of her pussy such that she immediately starts to climax. But it isn't a cumming climax. It's a suspended orgasm, her pussy oozing juice over Luke so that every millimeter of his cock is inside her, deep and totally immersed. Lucinda enjoys this total fuck completely.

Bakeem brings Natalie to the same state. His fucking is harder though, rapid deep strokes made possible by the normal extra large cock he has. Luke is not possessed of normal, and so he needs to make his thrusting focused on dragging against the cunt he fucks as opposed to shooting his cock into the back of it. Natalie is settled, as is Lucinda, into the fact that there is no other man in the room that she would rather have inside her for the final stretch. The girls are fucked, albeit differently, for what seems like forever. They are grateful that the boys are in no hurry to cum as they have orgasm after orgasm so quick in succession that it feels like a prolonged single climax. The wetness of their cunts is undeniable, a definite factor in the boys' not cumming, too little contact, even for Luke, as the sludge pits become fuck ponds. Both men withdraw, use their tongues to dry the pussies under them, and then send thick cock into the dry cunts with a renewed focus on their own orgasms.

Luke and Lucinda are the first to reach a simultaneous orgasm. There is no withdrawing as Luke shoots gallons of cum into Lucinda. They are both wise enough to know that there are processes that will counter the effects of his load up inside her, and so she lets him do what he's probably done only a few times before. A condom would have never meant climax inside her, his erection too large for any on the market. She cums again in buckets; twice during his orgasm, and they simply enjoy the extended moment. They hug, kiss for the longest time as Luke enjoys thrusting his softening cock into her, something that brings him to another climax, less wet, before he finally removes his thickness from Lucinda. They immediately position themselves so that they can suck each other clean before making their way to the shower.

Bakeem and Natalie only reach their climax once the others are in the shower. They are loud and unapologetic as Bakeem, who has managed to withdraw and suit up, therefore extending their fuck, shoots his black cock so hard into Natalie that she has several orgasms before him finally cums. He can't be quiet as he cums for three minutes, the condom straining under his load. She holds him inside her and gyrates her waist in small circles, Bakeem getting three more full erections and cumming three more times before they eventually accept that they've already tempted fate three times, the condom designed for single use as are all the others. He removes his cock, and the condom, ties it, and wraps it in some Kleenex before sending his cock into Natalie for a final round. He cums dry and so just lies with his cock inside her until the others exit and let them know that the shower is available...

The sun finally makes a full appearance. It's been raining for four straight days, and were it not for the fuck-fest the group of eight had been having, this might have proven to be a rather frustrating time. But explorations of Chinese culture were replaced by discoveries of South African vagina, the explorers from two continents making absolutely sure that they left no part of the pussy unchartered. One cunt had found itself somewhat neglected though. While Uchell had engaged rather enthusiastically with any cock that found its way to her, none of them had ventured inside her with more than a tongue or a finger or few. She didn't mind really, everyone thoroughly enjoying the show offered up by her and whoever she happened to be sucking.

Jabari looks to where Bakeem and Natalie are sleeping. On the same mattress, Lucinda is locked in Luke's arms. They're also sleeping. He looks at Nate and the other guys, all of them trying to process what has probably happened. They all know of course, and they also notice that Uchell is conspicuously absent. Ethan catches a look between Nate and Jabari and then all three look to the door. The three are not sure for a minute but then after quickly getting the necessary admin of teeth brushing and face washing out of the way, the threesome slips out of the room without waking the others who are clearly all fucked out. They head in the direction of the girl's room, hoping in the warm morning that this is where Uchell is, possibly taking care of her own necessary admin.

Uchell stands under the private shower in their room, a luxury that cost them a little extra as did their private room, the dorm setup not appealing to the privileged trio, as it didn't to the Americans. Luke and Ethan were in a dorm though, but with four other English lads so it worked out to the same thing. Their roommates had been missing for most of their trip anyway... The water is warm, but not hot. Uchell watches the city rising through the slits in the wall, the smell of cinnamon from her shampoo coupled with the visuals of outside making her feel like she was showering on the street in full view of the locals. This thought brings a smile to her face as she imagines herself being admired by scores of men as they make their way to work. Being foreign has as much an exotic appeal to the locals as it does to the foreigner themselves.

The knock on the door isn't loud. But the walls are so thin that it sounds as though Jabari is knocking on the bathroom door. This startles Uchell a little but she quickly gets her bearings and reaches for the towel. She doesn't bother to ask who it is, assuming that one of the girls had forgotten her key and was also now in need of the shower and some shampoo. Instead, three men stand in the doorway looking like they've lost their way and she is the only one who can guide them back from whence they come. Ethan holds out two cups of coffee, Jabari and Nate sipping on theirs. All six eyes ask to be let in. Their eyes beg to be let in to the room with the freshly washed pussy that can be unwrapped with one tug on the towel. Her hair drips onto her delicate shoulders and all three men have the incredible desire to lick up the droplets.

The coffee tastes better than the paper cups would have had Uchell believe. She drinks it without too much concern that her towel is having the same effect on the cocks around her that the coffee is having on her. Nate is the first to finish his coffee and also the first to initiate the action they had come for. Uchell expects the move but still it catches her by surprise. Nate's hand goes immediately under the towel and rests on her thigh. Jabari and Ethan look away briefly, in case Uchell's coffee becomes airborne. Instead, she takes one long sip to empty her cup, opening her legs at the same time, offering a complete view of her pussy, still wet from the shower. The other cups are emptied loudly.

Nate's long finger makes short work of finding the inside of her pussy. Uchell lets herself fall all the way back onto the floor, unwrapping the towel as she does so that by the time she is flat on her back the towel is perfectly placed between her back and the floor. Nate's finger goes all the way into her, her legs spread so that the other boys get a view of the ultimate prize. Ethan and Jabari are soon on the floor on either side of her, rubbing her thighs, working their hands closer and closer to where Nate's finger is working. Jabari runs his index in soft circles over her clit. Ethan wets his finger in her mouth and then sends it into her vagina along with Nate's.

The two fingers inside her don't move

together. They work against each other, fighting for space inside her and sawing each other in half. Uchell cannot process the rhythm because it's nonexistent. The pleasure of the battle ensuing in her cunt on the other hand is unmistakable. Who needs order when your pussy feels like a million slithering cobras are having a wrestling match inside it, which ends with the serpents exploding in a billion bubbles of pleasure? Jabari soon finds an angle of entry and there are three cobras caught in the dance of death inside Uchell's pussy, now hooded by a superimposed clitoris.

Ethan moves back just enough so that his cock lines up with her face. Uchell has only to turn slightly to the side for the cock to find her mouth. She sucks on his cock with the same delicious giving that the fingers are displaying on her cunt. Her ear is to the ground, her neck taking absolutely no strain thanks to her dancing background, and Ethan is able to fuck her remarkably deep mouth with ease, practically his entire cock disappearing into her. The surprise is obvious on his face for several thrusts. As soon as he accepts that the impossible is indeed possible though he starts to really send his meat into her, fucking her mouth harder now than all three fingers in her cunt.

Jabari doesn't need much more

motivation to strategically position his own cock as well. He allows Ethan a few more strokes before he taps his cock on the side of Uchell's face. She takes a last indulgent suck of the entire cock as she pulls it deep into her mouth, keeps it there with her lips, presses her tongue against it as if to lodge it in place, and then moves her head slowly off it, fighting her own movement with her tongue until eventually turning her head in the direction of Jabari's waiting cock releases Ethan's meat completely. Jabari's cock is in her mouth before she has time to close it and she immediately sucks the hard dark meat into her mouth. She sucks Jabari's cock a little harder than she did Ethan's, his meat thicker, tougher, and juicier. Jabari's cock also somehow tastes better.

Ethan's cock starts to go limp, either out of jealousy, or irritation at what is obviously some serious tonguing. It's he who now slaps his meat on the side of Uchell's face. Jabari understands his frustration and slowly extracts just enough of his dick out of her mouth so that she can turn and face upwards. She opens her mouth a little wider, allowing Ethan to slip his soft cock into it. She sucks both cocks, one hard, the other getting there quickly now in the warmth of her mouth and under the careful guidance of her tongue. Both cocks are soon allies in her mouth, working together to give each other pleasure by staying close enough to one another for Uchell to have the necessary room to play. Her tongue and lips work together to ensure that the team effort is rewarded. Jabari and Ethan fuck her mouth at comfortable diagonals, her arms through their legs, her hands resting on their toned butts, squeezing.

Nate's cock has gone unattended for long enough and he lifts Uchell up slowly so as not to abort the cocks from her mouth, but rather to encourage them to vacate the space. Ethan and Jabari create the space needed between them for Nate to park his cock over Uchell's mouth, his face between her thighs. She pulls the cock into her mouth using both hands as Nate goes hard and deep into her pussy. Once she settles comfortably into the sixty-nine Uchell takes Ethan and Jabari's cocks in her hands. Nate's fucking into her mouth, his sucking on her pussy, and Uchell's firm strokes on the rods she's palmed reach a remarkable equilibrium of both pace and pressure, and they move as though they're one being.

Uchell brings her legs up, squeezing Nate's head between her thighs before raising her legs skyward. Ethan and Jabari pull her legs towards themselves and then lift slightly, Nate having to raise his own head, as the pussy beneath him suddenly seems to levitate. His cock sinks deeper into her mouth though as his back bends, and Uchell takes the excess meat into her throat by letting out a long steady breath through her nose and willing the muscles in the back of her mouth to relax. Ethan releases the leg in his hand and Nate relaxes his thrusts as his back straightens a little. Uchell appreciates this relief and shows her gratitude by allowing Ethan complete entry into her ass when his cock is suddenly on her hole, and then inside it. Ethan is careful to thrust as gently into her ass as Nate is nibbling on her cunt to avoid a collision between Nate's mouth and his extra large nuts.

The leg in Jabari's hand comes down onto Ethan, who now reclines so that his body forms a right angle with Uchell's as his cock moves around inside her ass. Both her legs rest on Ethan as he fucks her, pushing her pussy towards Nate, still hungrily devours it. Jabari reluctantly releases his cock from her hold and Uchell's hands are suddenly both free. She grabs Nate's ass and lets him know that he can resume his thrusting since she has the control afforded her by her free hands, to push him up should he go too deep. He lifts his back much higher; his cock deeper just as Jabari gets to Uchell's waist and straddles her. Nate keeps his cock in her mouth and does a complete one-eighty so that he now looks away from the scene playing out on Uchell's cunt and in her ass. As Nate continues his assault on her mouth, Jabari sinks his meat into Uchell's cunt. Her pussy practically pulls the penis into itself, grateful for the first cock to finally enter her.

Jabari's cock is thick and heavy inside her, the force of Ethan in her ass adding to the sensation of being filled completely. On his knees, Jabari cannot really thrust into her, and bending forward so that he can gain the leverage to make thrusting possible would put his face in Nate's ass. So he drops his cock deep into her, as deep as it will go, and then rocks back in forth rigorously, providing the entire penetrated portion of her vagina with the leverage to vibrate under the intense sensation. Nate knows that the gasping that has Uchell loosen her grip on his cock has everything to do with the cock in her cunt, and so he too decides that it might be time to get the pussy to purr a little under his persuasion. He lifts off of her and strokes his meat as he kneels next to Jabari, letting him know that he'd like a go.

He is given a gap, but not until Jabari has leaned forward completely, kissed Uchell, and given her cunt several solid thrusts. Every inch of Jabari is inside her, his powerful thrusts bringing her surprisingly close to orgasm. He lifts his mouth from hers and allows her to make the state of her cunt known audibly. He silences her again with his lips, fills her with cock in several more solid thrusts, and then abruptly lifts out of her completely as much to avoid his own ejaculation as to halt her own climax. He keeps his lips on hers as he moves his body all the way around and gives Nate access to the vibrating vagina. Nate is inside her in one movement, his thrusting beginning immediately. Uchell is again given the freedom of her mouth as she pants at Nate's penetration, Jabari making his cock ready to go where his mouth just was, and Ethan exiting her ass and dressing his cock for a dive into her cunt, just as soon as Nate will allow this, of course.

Nate doesn't give up Uchell's pussy until he has satisfied himself that she knows his name. He uses a series of various strokes to write his name on the inside of her pussy so absolutely that the name leaves her mouth in whispers despite the presence of Jabari's cock between her lips. He withdraws just before he signs the inner walls of her pussy in semen, a move that frustrates him, but delights Ethan who has already spent a little too much time running his own familiar fingers over his own cock. Nate lets his dick regain some composure before joining his fellow American in Uchell's mouth. Her cunt is now exposed to a ten-inch English invasion courtesy of Ethan, who places his cock on her pussy, plays around with his head in the entrance for a bit, and then runs his shaft swiftly into her until even his balls seem to enter her. Her mouth opens just wide enough for the ebony cocks to drop another half inch into it.

Jabari and Nate enjoy her mouth. They watch as Ethan rams his meat into her again and again, occasionally resulting in a widening of the gap they occupy, allowing both cocks to drop even further. They don't need to thank him; their rock-hard dicks evidence enough of gratitude. Ethan sends his cock up into Uchell as though he were trying to find something he'd misplaced in the far reaches of her pussy. He hides his face in her neck, biting into the soft flesh he finds there, enjoying her delicate, feminine touch. The feel of her sends blood to his already overwrought cock and the meat strains against itself but manages to grow a little more. The thick swelling cock pushes against Uchell's pussy and sends her into a delirium where her body is unsure of what her mind is telling her is an orgasm. It isn't...

The cocks in her mouth start to dress

the back of her mouth in a light cream and so Jabari makes a quick escape. He lets his cock hang ten before suiting it up and positioning himself in Ethan's original spot. For this to happen though, Ethan has to pivot so that his body forms a cross with Uchell's, who has to bend her knees over Jabari, who has to slide underneath her almost, before his cock finds the warmth of her ass. The angle of entry for Jabari is comfortable for both him and Uchell. Her pussy takes an incredibly huge amount of added cock pressure from Ethan though in his new position. Her cunt isn't complaining though, and Nate, in her mouth, is pleased with the spectacle.

Nate takes a few more dips into her mouth before initiating the awkward removal of Jabari from his position. Jabari slithers out, redresses his cock and then stands in wait for Ethan, who has had more than his fair share of pussy. Nate is inside her ass as Ethan finally lets go of her vagina and allows Jabari a dip. The new condom seems to have reenergized his cock and Jabari is soon sending vibrations through her that make her pussy feel like it has its own high-frequency radio station. Inside her ass, Nate matches these vibrations, beat for beat. Ethan removes the condom from his cock before plunging his tool into her mouth. Uchell is in heaven, three cocks fully working every part of her that has any potential to be worked by dick.

Ethan realizes that Uchell's mouth is as hot as her cunt and leans over her face, his arms and feet on the floor in a pushup position. He holds himself up like this as he thrusts into her mouth and fucks her steadily while her cunt and ass are dressed with a little color. Jabari has full cognizance now too of what it was that made Ethan so possessive of Uchell's pussy, the vacuum keeping so tight a grip on his cock that he has no idea who is fucking who. Nate rests comfortably in her ass, thrusting at a steady pace with no real rush to get anywhere. All three of them again find that perfect pace, that perfect pressure, and then work themselves so close to orgasm that it hurts when all of them withdraw from the holes they occupy, almost simultaneously.

Jabari sends his cock back into her pussy, a reflex action almost. Nate and Ethan just watch, pulling on their own cocks and then changing their condoms unnecessarily. Jabari now lifts himself high off of Uchell, but not high enough to entirely leave her cunt. The height of his lift though sends an inescapable wave, an almost shock wave through her every time he drops down and shoots his long cock back inside her. He seems to almost jump off her pussy and then plow back in, over and over again. And each time she lets out a yelp. The pleasure is an intense pounding that rushes through her in waves so that soon she is on her way to climax, with no possible comprehension of what could cause her to veer off the path. But then Jabari's thrusting settles into the rear end of her pussy and he lets out a sound that can only mean he's beaten her to the finish line.

Fortunately, soldier Nate is on standby. He shoots into her pussy so soon after Jabari's exit that the lapse in time between them is negligible. Uchell loses just a little of her momentum but Nate is skilled enough to know just how to guide her back onto the yellow brick road. He finds her depths and settles himself there. His strokes are deep and circular, touching his cock to every part of her vagina as he draws her closer to climax than Jabari did. But again no sooner has she started to see the finish line and he too is releasing the guttural noises that let the room know that this man too is down. Like Jabari, he is too satisfied with his own orgasm to feel too bad for her, knowing that Private Ethan will pick up the baton and see the filly to the finish.

Ethan is back in her pussy with bells on. He and his cock display the kind of gusto that lets the entire room know that he will do exactly what his cock has been mandated to. He too sends every inch of himself into her and then lets it find a comfortable resting place. He then takes his cock on a trip around the world in wide circles that stretch the opening of her pussy for moments before it wraps snuggly back over his penis. When his cock can go no deeper, and his circles get no wider, he settles into the maximum scope of his motion and works with renewed intent on her pussy, having let it know what the road to the end will constitute. Every aspect of the journey now perfectly lay out; Ethan takes the reign and rides his filly home.

Despite the clarity of vision, the dash to the end isn't swift. Ethan is still in her pussy long after Nate and Jabari have undressed their dicks. They've made their way to her mouth again and offered her flaccid cock to keep her occupied up top while Ethan takes care of her below. Ethan's face is again in her neck, his teeth, tongue and lips on it. Hiding for reasons only he knows he creates longer and longer strokes, pulling on the inside of her vagina as he extends the reach and then the drag of his cock. Uchell knows that it's going to be any second now, but Ethan starts to flip the script on her cunt so many times that she starts to doubt it despite everything her cunt is telling her.

Ethan drives back into his original resting place again, widening the circles again, showing her the Promised Land just beyond the river that has started to flow between her thighs. She needs to cross this river, wanting to take herself there in frustration despite Ethan's cock still being in her pussy. He senses this and allows himself to see his own finish. He knows now that he has taken her to where he needed to so that they can be sure to cross over together. The drag is again extended and the inside of her cunt becomes a chalkboard upon which Ethan starts to chalk the completeness that would be her orgasm. It comes in waves, then tremors, then violent convulsions that would have been mistaken for a medical emergency had she not been screaming ecstatically throughout. Ethan's cock shoots off a massive load mid her orgasm and the two climaxes fuse for the minute or so it takes them to rise and fall on the crescent wave of foreign fucking bliss...

It's impossible for all four of them to shower together, the cubicle ridiculously small. There is not an awkward moment past between them though as one by one they go into the tiny room and clean up, the rest left enjoying the sudden breeze blowing into the window along with the sounds of a city suddenly wide awake.

They laugh about the total reckless abandon of the last few days and vow never to mention it at each other's weddings or on each other's Facebook walls as they exchange social media details. All clean and fresh, they leave the room and go to wake the others.

The room still smells of sex when they enter, but the window is wide open and the breeze is going some ways in alleviating the scent. The four, who look even more like couples now, are also washed up already, the girls in fresh T-shirts courtesy of Bakeem. They decide that breakfast will be best enjoyed out in the sun and make their way out of the room. They know they won't be in the room together again, everyone resuming their original itineraries immediately after breakfast, but they are not sad. Silent pacts are made again to speak naught of this experience to anyone but each other and especially not to make social media a platform for incriminating innuendos. They're all too clever for that though, and with Bakeem and Luke seemingly totally taken with Natalie and Lucinda, whatever wild and wicked associations were left of this experience belonged exclusively to Uchell and her musketeers. Breakfast goes down very well...

5 BITE ME ONCE

Prologue

It isn't often that a man begs to be bitten, but when the teeth belong to Beth Jones, they practically roll on the floor beseeching. Beth knows she's perfected an art, and fortunately for her, she discovers that she isn't the only one when one night one of her trysts decides to bite back.

Beth Jones is a perfect ballerina. In the hallowed halls of the New York City Ballet, she is almost idealized by her contemporaries. It isn't difficult to see why, perfect form, perfect shape, perfect technique, flawless skin, and deliciously red lips against her milky hue off-set boldly by her pitch black hair; her list of perfections was endless. But, as many of her past and present lovers know, Beth's best asset was just behind those rosebud lips. Her most delicious feature was her teeth....

It isn't hard to imagine that someone with a life as rigid as that of a ballerina would seek an escape of sorts that involved losing herself somewhat in physical revelry. But the area Beth found herself lost in was nothing like the damsels in distress she often played to packed theatres. No, Beth Jones was a little bit of a sadist. She found that she was able to marry pain and pleasure so intimately that pretty soon relationships were not necessary, just bodies.

After a string of very satisfied sexual partners, Beth finds herself in the bed of an Arabian photographer, just passing through as many do in New York. And when Armin turns the tables, taking nibble after nibble out of sweet Beth, only then does she realize what it is to truly lose oneself....

Once Bitten... (Bite Marks...)

The hot air escaping Beth's mouth hits Jet's balls as though she were trying to steam up a windowpane. But, just as the heat expands his sack, tiny Beth takes the tender flesh between her teeth and bites onto it. Jet grabbing her head, wanting to push her away just as the pleasure replaces the pain and he practically wipes her face with his dick. He exhales hard. She can only fit one of his balls in her mouth at a time, so she runs her teeth over one testicle, biting but not until the oval lump gives way to his tender bits again, and she bites. He winces, and then moans. A firm grip on her head again, and his cock again thinking it was a windshield wiper for her face.

Beth can do this for hours, enjoying not just the raw scent of cock and cum, the smell of sweat and cigarettes, the taste of dick in her mouth with the assurance of cock up her cunt before bedtime. But also absolutely loving the responses delivered by the body, she tortures with her teeth. Her five-foot frame makes the ballerina a very compact assailant, able to contort herself into the most delicious positions, both for the viewing pleasure of her partner and for ease of access to the places she wants to sink her teeth into.

She knows if she's going to get a few good bites she's going to need to offer up a distraction. Her fleshy pink pussy is the perfect sacrifice. She sits Jet on the recliner, dropping it ever so slightly so that he almost lies on his back but not, a half-seated position. She climbs over him from above his head, a perfect 69 except that her height allows her to almost kneel on the rest behind his shoulders, her pussy in prime position in front of him so that he only needs to lift his head off the rest to taste her cunt. From this position, she can't reach his sack, but from his nipples, all the way down past his shaft and along his waistline, that's an open playing field. Beth proceeds to play her favorite game.

Jet's moans are loud. He silences himself by sinking his tongue into Beth's available vagina. She receives him willingly. He holds her in position by wrapping his arms over her thighs, a move that allows her to drop into his chest without fear of falling. She sticks her tongue out and wraps the pink flesh over the head of the cock in front of her. Her tongue circles the thick head, licking it as though it were made of vanilla and hot fudge. Jet's mouth, nose, and tongue all fuck the tiny cunt they've been awarded, a gesture of appreciation. Beth follows by taking as much dick in her mouth as she can without suffocating herself.

The sucks are hard, slow movements that almost rock Jet into a daze. It's during this horny haze, when all he can manage is to pull Beth's pussy over his nose in an attempt to stop himself from breathing, to distract himself from cumming. This is when Beth makes the transition from sucking to nibbling. Her teeth sink into his shaft in uniform patterns, at constant intervals until she reaches the tender head, at which point she releases the bite and slides her lips and tongue back down as far as she can go.

How much of his decent-sized dick is swallowed is essentially up to Jet, but he is caught in a catch-22. The more of his shaft he feeds her, a simple matter of releasing his hold on her thighs and grabbing her waist so that he can edge her forward onto his needy cock, the more shaft she has to bite on, on her way back up. Also, he loses the delicious cunt he's feeding on. What's a man to do? Of course, the better choice would be to do both, not possible at the same time though.

Naturally, his dick takes precedence, and he is soon completely swallowed by Beth. He braces himself for the nibbles as he pulls her pussy towards his mouth, his tongue finding the inside of her cunt just as the first tingle etches its way through his thighs, then his groin. Mercifully, Beth knows not to nibble on his uncovered dick-head. This cock-suck-pussy-fuck seesaw goes on for as long as Jet's arms can hold out, which isn't very long as soon as the first indications of climax start to trace up his length from his balls.

Ever the gentleman, he lets the petite beauty know that he's close. He does this knowing that she knows though; she's always had a sense for his explosion. She etches down onto his cock, settling his head in her throat, and then, with the poise that only she can muster, she slides off of him in a 180 until she is perfectly placed between his legs, his so-close-to-cumming-he-can't-stand-it dick still locked down tight between her rosy lips. He reaches for her head and slowly pulls a smiling Beth off his dick.

The moment seems to suspend as he takes in the sheer magnitude of what Beth has just managed. That he has not blown his load all over her face is nothing short of a miracle. The delicate beauty really is a mistress of the cock, her skill with a dick belied by her innocence. It is in fact this innocent façade, this damsel in distress appearance, that seems to be a side effect of playing so many roles to this effect in her real life as a prima ballerina at the New York City Ballet that makes Beth Jones such a turn on.

Again, she slides onto his cock, again taking it all into her mouth and again biting her way to the top. The torture is enough for Jet to drizzle a little jizz onto Beth's tongue a few times. Still, she goes down for more; she takes his meat into her mouth, enjoying the process almost as much as he does. In fact, Beth relishes cock in her mouth. And she absolutely loves flesh between her teeth. She bites into him now with the deliberate intention of drawing fluid from him. Thankfully, she isn't after blood.

He relaxes into an almost climax as Beth's teeth find his balls again, and then his thigh, then his balls again, now pulled tightly in the delicate sack that houses them due to the fullness of his erection. She has a way of sucking and biting at the same time, confusing his cock so much that it soon forgets the recent urgency of his ejaculation. He starts to stroke his cock now, knowing that soon he's going to need to attend to it anyway, if Beth doesn't. She is yet to disappoint him though so he continues to indulge her little fetish, easing up on his own masturbating so as not to shoot his load in her face as opposed to up some of the other places she's let him drop a load in the past.

When her teeth find the spot between his sack and his ass, Jet's legs part involuntarily, a sensation that throws him slightly. He lays back and accepts this assault, giving himself the proverbial 'minute' he assumes will be necessary for him to adjust to it. His hand is soon on his dick again as the 'adjustment' happens. Why the fuck hadn't anybody pointed out this hotspot to him before. Beth has just confirmed her fuck-goddess status, something for which she deserves a great reward. Every time he's had the pleasure of fucking her, she's never failed to surprise him.

By the time she lifts her head from between his legs, his cock is wrapped in a thin yellow film and smells like a cross between banana and vanilla. She shows her appreciation for the thoughtfulness that must have gone into the flavored condom by taking the yellow rod in her mouth and sliding her rosy red lips up and down the full length of it until again Jet pulls her off him, too close to take another descent of the hot mouth on his dick. He pulls her up and then grabs her legs, splitting her over the recliner, positioning her on his meat.

Beth wraps her arms around his neck and sinks her head into his chest, her nipples rubbing against his hairy torso as his cock fills her with banana and the scent of sponge cake. She relaxes herself into his grip and allows him to move her up and down his dick, surrendering herself to his rhythm. Her grip tightens as stroke after stroke Jet's cock finds that spot inside her that has eluded lesser lovers. He knows just where to find it and he knows just when to hit it. Every time his cock finds the back of her vagina, it pulls a little more cunt juice out, giving it greater access on the next advancement, stretching the back of her pussy even further. Jet fucks her this way until she lets him know that she is now close.

The thought of her climax sends Jet into frenzy. He practically swallows her breasts, one at a time, licking the nipples gently as the cup fills his mouth. He enjoys the idea of getting her to this point, relishing even more the fact that he has his rod inside her with such full authority that he is the only man on her mind. His jock ego needs to make this mental note. She confirms his virility by announcing her impending orgasm.

With her satisfaction now guaranteed, Jet lets his hands drop to his side, Beth dropping onto the full length of his penis. A rush of cold air flutters across her chest where the saliva from Jet's mouth now cools in the absence of his tongue. She holds on to him even tighter as he grips the sides of the recliner. It's time to race for the finish. He allows his cock to build momentum with a few slow strokes. His cock doesn't miss her g-spot once. As soon as he's dick is ready for explosion, he starts to lift Beth off the recliner with his dick. Stroke after pounding stroke, he pushes her into the air and then brings her back, his own ass lifting of the chair as he pushes through Beth's cunt with his short, thick cock. Beth's pussy flows with joy at this rapid escalation of fucking pleasure.

Her climax is audible. He let the last of her moans of gratitude leave her mouth before he takes her ass in his hands and pushed her down on his dick again, all the way, her vagina squeezing the last shots of pleasure out of his meat. He moves her around his cock gently as he loses the last bits of restraint and let's himself go. His own climax is a series of husky breaths and a whispered 'fuck'. An hour later, they're both asleep in their own apartments, alone in their own beds.

Beth likes that; she can go for months without fucking and then indulge herself with any one of the men on her list of fuck-buddies who probably sit waiting with baited breath for the call from Biting Beth. She tries to keep her escapades far enough apart for her to feel like she's just had a sparse set of one-night stands as opposed to a string of random bedfellows. This eases her conscience sufficiently.

The memories of Jet and his jock cock flood her mind as she gets ready to go to work. She opts for the shower, knowing that if she lay in the bath she might overly indulge her need to touch herself that results from her very vivid imagination. The warm water over her follows the contours of her body, tracing a path to where her fingers have already parted her pussy and made a careful entry. She touches herself with the deliberateness of an expert surgeon, knowing exactly what pressure will result in what sensation. With the little time she has before she has to be out of her apartment, she goes for the sprint and not the marathon.

Beth all but collapses on the shower floor as she brings herself to climax. The water washes her orgasm down the drain, and she's soon biting on an apple as she is locking her front door. The walk to the subway is a jolly 'yes I did get it all this morning' spring, and by the time she's into her first warm-up exercises, everyone in the studio can tell that she's probably had a very good night. She giggles to herself, knowing that they couldn't possibly know how good. After all, everyone assumes that a good night for little Beth is a date where the guy holds her hand....

Armin is a photographer. The current assignment he has is simple enough, a few action shots of a ballet rehearsal followed by stills of the actual performance and that was it. It was going to be a quick in to New York, and then he would fly back to London to hand the shots to his boss for use in a photo editorial for the performing arts. This assignment was nothing like some of the more high profile jobs he'd just recently completed. There was a function in the royal palace in Jordan and then the Whitehouse assignment. The men displaying remarkable athleticism, throwing and catching delicate flat-chested waifs before letting them touch the surface of the rehearsal room hardly made for the grit he had preferred for most of his career.

Set up in a corner of the room so as to protect himself and his equipment from the events across the floor, Armin makes himself comfortable with a rather good cup of coffee offered to him by the pianist. Everyone else ignores the photographer for the most part, which makes his job of being inconspicuous easier. He knows that you always get the best shots, the most real representations of people when they don't think you're shooting. He gets through several frames before anything really interesting happens. Armin discovers very quickly that there are few things more interesting than Beth Jones today, given that she is dancing the lead in Copellia, the ballet company's rather unusual offering for Christmas.

Beth isn't late as she glides into the room with the arrogance of someone who has mastered what ninety percent of women will only ever aspire to briefly in their lives, having their hopes dashed by inherent inadequacies very early on. She finds a place near the back of the room and warms up at the bar while the corps completes its rehearsal, half the men and a few of the women distracted by her. It's not a sexually charged distraction really, more a reverence. This really was a whole other world, where something that would be frowned upon as fragile and weak in the real world is now the thing to aspire towards in this environment of exaggerated contradictions.

The reflection fed back to Beth from the many mirrors is a perfect replica from head to toe of the ballerina. Her entire warm-up is fluid, and it appears that she is already dancing. Only when the choreographer, an aged European beauty with a body that matches her surroundings perfectly, calls Beth over and welcomes her, only then does Armin realize that he has actually been staring at the milky sprite throughout her half-stretch half-dance.

He recovers from the moment and proceeds with his job, still staring at Beth, but this time through the lenses of his camera. The pink of her skirt gathers between her thighs and is released as she lifts her leg in the air in large circles, exposing the outline of what Armin imagines to be very tight pussy. Hand after hand grabs her so close to her cunt that surely the thought of a stray finger must occur to her; although if it does, she doesn't show it. The hours go by quickly and the room gives itself a round of applause for its own performance as the choreographer thanks the dancers and they start to file out.

Beth allows herself to check out the stranger in the corner only once she has completely discarded her role and thrown a pair of leggings on, wrapping herself in a shawl. She watches him pack up and then pour himself another unsolicited cup of coffee, the pianist already gone. A few of the guys get lost in a series of jumps; an exercise Armin assumes is the equivalent of a group of peacocks displaying their feathers. Beth is unmoved, having seen it all a thousand times before. Ignoring the mock practice, she pours herself a cup of coffee and asks the photographer the one question that has always meant he was about to get laid. "Can I see those?" she asks him, pointing to the camera. He obliges her, showing her the tiny shots on the camera's display.

They get through a few shots and then Armin suggests she wait to see them in the article. He points out that you only get a real appreciation for the picture once it's blown up. They finish their coffee and turn off the lights, being the last two left in the studio. Armin is playing with the thought of fucking a ballerina, and Beth is wondering if he tastes as good as he looks. The front door to the building, the main exit, comes up and he pushes it open for her, knowing that he might lose the moment if she disappears into the New York rush on the other side of the doors. "I could show you the pictures on my laptop if you like." He says this as he holds the door open, expecting her to say no and hurry off, but also knowing from experience that subjects were too arrogant to really engage with a photographer so when they did it had nothing to do with the pictures.

The tiny loft that belongs to the publication that Armin works for is a short walk from where they are, and so they slip through the crowd and make for the warmth of the tiny functional space. It was designed for little more than sleeping, everything in the extreme open except for the bathroom, and nothing more than a desk, a bed and a sofa. The kitchen area is well equipped though but also just. The entire arrangement is comfortable enough for anyone on assignment in New York to get things done and stylish enough for anyone looking to get fucked on assignment in New York to be able to do so impressively.

The warmth inside makes the shawl over Beth's shoulders unnecessary,

Armin's coat also discarded. He offers a coffee, which she accepts, and then they sit at the desk as he plugs his camera into the laptop and creates a slideshow for Beth's benefit. He moves in behind her to help her navigate back and forth over the shots she wants to see again. She apologizes a few times for not having showered and he points to the bathroom in half-jest. His hands rest on her shoulders presumptuously as she admires the pictures of the other dancers. He admires hers, and she feigns modesty. Beth had seemed flat chested in the rehearsal, but close up Armin notices the perfect round of her breasts, attention drawn to them by the nipples that seem to have grown significantly since his hands found the back of her neck.

That they would fuck was now obvious. When they would fuck was what had both of them caught in a bit of a dilemma. The complication that could arise if things went badly would not only jeopardize Armin's job assignment but also Beth's, since she would need to be able to perform without distraction. If it went well, it might still backfire, the resultant orgasms, or memories thereof, offering as strong a distraction, albeit a different one. Beth's eyes meet Armin's in the now black computer screen, and without words, it is decided that they're already both in the same room and they had known exactly what both of them wanted when the request was made to view the pics and the offer for a private viewing was both made and accepted.

The lady in Beth has her undress as she walks in the direction of the shower. Armin follows closely behind her. They're both completely naked by the time the hot water juts through the spout and over them. Beth's hands fall on Armin's chest, sinking somewhat into the hairy depth. His olive skin is almost completely covered by the most beautifully rich auburn carpet. She had anticipated some hair but his was exceptional. The smell of honey and almonds immediately envelopes the cubicle, just as Beth's eyes fall on Armin's dick brushing the side of her thigh.

She takes the shower gel from him and soaps up, Armin already white. They make quick work of the shower, no real touching except for the odd straying dick against the milky dancer. Beth resolves immediately not to try anything too risqué since the last thing she needs is an awkward end to an afternoon on which she has decided to simply indulge a curiosity. She really doesn't want a long drawn out bite fest, although it would be nice, but the dick being dried in front of her looks to be all that would be needed to satisfy her spontaneous urge. The cock is long. What is lost in girth is well compensated for in length. Besides, if she behaves today, she can hope for a follow-up before he leaves, at which time she can turn the fucking into more of a meal.

She stares briefly at her face in the mirror before Armin moves in and moves her out of the bathroom to the bed. She crawls up onto the large cushioned surface and hasn't made it to the far end of it when a hot tongue settles in her crack and immediately finds her asshole. She throws herself flat on the bed in surprise, the tongue immediately finding her again and digging in, deeper this time, the bed underneath her giving her no way of escaping. Armin grabs her under her thighs and parts her legs. His tongue finds her cunt and his licks become successive laps from pussy to ass, long licks from front to back with occasional kisses straying onto her back.

Beth pulls a few of the silk pillows towards herself, resting a couple under her breasts and losing her face in a few. She breathes easily through the silk but feels sufficiently hidden from the man behind her. Her ass is raised off the bed and her pussy brought back down onto thick lips and a hot tongue. Armin has now turned onto his back for better cunt access. Beth, still on her stomach, fucks the tongue that makes light work of her vagina.

Beth is in mid-orgasm when suddenly her cunt is invaded by cock. She can't believe that she didn't even realize that Armin had stolen his tongue from inside her. She cannot believe that he had the ability to create a suspended orgasm such that she felt even in the absence of his fleshy pussy-licker that it was inside her. She essentially fucked the thought of his tongue as he slid out from under her, suited his cock up and ran it into the waiting cunt.

Armin rests both his hands on Beth's head as they flatten onto the bed. She is flat on her stomach save for the cushions under her breasts, and he is flat on her back with his dick deep enough inside her pussy for him to fuck her without needing to move. He gets deep inside her despite her legs being closed together, something made possible by his long penis. It isn't thick by no account, but the length of it, easily twelve or thirteen inches, allows this position to be remarkably satisfying both ways. He gets to fuck the shit out of her with the feeling of being all the way inside. And she gets the feeling of being totally fucked by an abnormally long schlong without having to deal with the awkwardness that would usually arise from being fucked by an abnormally long schlong.

They fuck for a good half an hour before Beth fills the room with the scent of her cunt's bliss. Armin lets himself go a minute or so later. Both of them are glad that they manage a decent conversation over coffee, still naked, in bed for a good hour post coital. It's a mature end to an unexpected and altogether pleasurable winter afternoon fuck. Armin sees Beth into a cab and they both disappear back into their own worlds.

The note in his hand surprises him as Beth all but ignores him throughout the rehearsal the next day. Her address is neatly written in the center of the yellow post-it. There were no hellos and no stares, at least not from her. Just the note inconspicuously handed to him as she replaced a coffee cup on the stand behind him near the piano. He stares at the address for as long as it takes everyone to leave and the janitor to remind him that it's snowing outside and he'd best be getting home.

He doesn't know what to expect when he walks up to the door of Beth's building. There were no arrangements, no times, and no calls, just the address. But here he was in front of the huge walk-up and so he may as well ring the bell. Again, there's no speaking, just the loud buzz and the door opening. Armin walks up the stairs, delaying his arrival at her door by avoiding the elevator. He's blood is warm by the time he gets onto the sixth floor and he finds her door. It's open....

She somehow knew that he wouldn't hesitate to come because the space is prepared for him. He hopes it's for him. The apartment is dark save for an array of candles that dot every corner and most of the surfaces. There's the sound of a log fire somewhere inside and Armin goes to find it. In the living room, he is greeted with the most beautiful scene: a feline figure, naked, sprawled in front of the flames on a scarlet tinted rug. He smiles and removes his scarf.

By the time he stands over her, he has discarded all of his clothing. Beth is on her knees, her hands wrapped around his ankles. She slides her fingers up his thighs and pries his legs a little further apart, returning her grip to his ankles. He looks at her questioningly but remains standing astride. Her body writhes and snakes, bends, stretches, contorts and flexes at his feet, and within seconds, he is mesmerized.

The soft kisses on his feet tickle. He giggles as she plants a few kisses on his ankles and then his calf. She kisses his knees and then gently bites into the side of them before licking the back of his knees. Signals in his brain relay a message to his cock that has it throbbing and jerking from side to side. By the time her lips find his inner thighs, his dick has stretched away from her towards the ceiling. It points away from her despite it wanting to make a connection with her. He laughs at his cock that seems insistent at fleeing the scene.

She hadn't really seen his sack before and the sight of the low-hanging testicles excites her. On her knees now, she can take the sack into her mouth without exerting herself. She licks his sack gently, lathering his balls in her own saliva. Armin points his dick down towards Beth, but that isn't what she wants yet. His cock is long enough for her to take three inches into her mouth anyway, sucking on this tip for a minute just to appease the owner of the serpent. Then it's back to the matter at hand.

She puts her arms between his legs and rests her hands on his ass. With this solid grip, she has perfect accessed to his balls, and she doesn't need to worry herself about falling. He just needs to concentrate on his own balance, but he seems to have it under control. Her licking resumes, then her sucking as she takes one of his eggs in her mouth. She takes the other one in her mouth, rolls her tongue over it and then sucks on the soft tissue. He moans his approval. She keeps up this sucking and licking, occasionally indulging his cock when he points it towards her mouth.

She sucks harder on the ball in her mouth, pulling on it as though she were intent on swallowing. He observes her cautiously. She lets her teeth take a gentle hold on the tissue, which rolls out of the grip, leaving her with the flesh of his sack between her teeth. She takes the gentlest bite, not hard enough for it to register as a bite. She goes for the ball again, and once it is safe in her mouth, she grips it between her teeth again, firmer this time so as not to lose it. He gives an even more cautious gaze, too late as she bite into his sack, sucks hard on the ball she's just bitten, rolls it around in her mouth and then rapidly licks the entire sack to erase the memory of the bite. He exhales relief.

She repeats this with the other ball, then back to the original. She alternates this way, building up the pressure of her bites, pushing the envelope, really testing his thresholds. He starts to dance, nervous. She giggles to herself, takes his dick in hand and pulls it into her mouth herself this time. He doesn't seem as keen to have his cock between her teeth as he had just a few minutes earlier. The tension turns her on even more. She lets herself strain up so that she takes seven inches into her mouth. His nervous look turns to admiration. She holds the dick in her mouth for as long as she can manage to hold her breath and then, taking a long breath through her nose she allows herself to fall to the ground, the dick seeming to follow her to the floor.

On her back, she is soon faced with dick in her face, her head caught between his thighs. Armin has pinned her between his legs. He drops his sack into her mouth, and then lifts it out just as she starts to get comfortable. He teases her this way for a while until she unexpectedly manages a grip on both his balls at the same time, with her teeth. He drops his sack all the way into her mouth in the hope that this will ease the pulling sensation. It does, but it has no effect on the biting. Beth starts to chew gently on the balls that have completely filled her mouth.

Armin bravely transforms his whimpering into husky grunts, breathing out loudly through his open mouth, from his throat. Beth rests her arms on the calf-muscles on both his legs and holds his heels down. He needs to move but is unsure of how to do it without hurting her. So he has no choice but to let her hurt him. Beth lets the balls go and takes a few good bites out of the sack before opening her mouth as wide as she can and exhaling hot air onto his reddened scrotum. He dangles the sack over the welcome air and then gently over her mouth as her lips close. She licks him tenderly.

Anticipating his next move, Beth opens her mouth whereupon a long thin cock makes its way inside. She lets him slide down to the maximum seven inches and then allows him a courteous couple of strokes as he gently fucks the back of her throat and rubs his cock against the sides of her mouth. She moves her head around slowly, ever so slightly until he is basically brushing her teeth with his dick. He's too lost in the sensation to realize that he's fallen full-length into her ambush. Her lips purse tightly shut; her teeth already on the meat of his shaft. He pushes down on her forehead with one hand. Her eyes warn him not to piss her off. They both laugh with their eyes as he motions surrender with both arms in the air.

She lets him withdraw, nibbling gently and then not so gently as he exits, until his head remains. He wonders if her teeth will dare for this most sensitive knob. She wonders if he thinks she might. There's a moment of panic, a moment of questioning and a moment of uncertainty. Then her tongue wraps around the underside of the head and licks it intensely as he pulls out of her completely. She turns her head to the side almost shyly and then takes a bite into his thigh. He immediately lifts his other leg over her and rolls onto his back.

She's on him like a banshee. With no effort from him, his dick is inside her, inching its way up her powerful pussy. As his cock snakes into her depths, she sinks her teeth into the sides of his muscular arms. He grabs her, almost throws her off him but is reminded by his cock of the pleasure between her thighs. He takes hold of her shoulders and forces her onto his cock, an almost ten-inch reprimand before she releases her teeth from his flesh. He eases his grip as they both look towards her pussy, his cock bending out of it, a good few inches still available for her. He dares her to bite him.

Beth pulls herself off his dick and makes for his neck, landing just under his ear. He screams, both for the pain, but also for his cock that now lies on his stomach having been spewed spontaneously from her vagina. Beth quickly goes for his lips, offering up a full passionate kiss, her tongue locks his inside his mouth. She takes back her tongue, biting his bottom lip as she sits up, and then arches back to offer him a view of her breasts. He takes them in hand briefly, and then goes for his cock which now aches for attention.

Beth goes in for another bite on the opposite side of his neck. This throws her balance enough for him to turn on his side. They face each other now, her one leg over him, the other pinned under him. Too late she tries to move. His cock is already inside her, and in the position they're in, there is nothing stopping him from impaling her on his dick. He could drive his shaft straight into her pussy and probably all the way to her heart. Again, he dares her to bite, but even before she does, he feeds her twelve slender inches. She has no way of moving as he drives his dick in and out of her in steady continuous movements. She wants to bite him. She thinks of drawing blood. But she can't breathe. She can hardly breathe as he continues to ram his cock as far inside her as it will go, the remainder of it bending outside her as he reaches the imaginary brick wall inside her.

He offers her a nipple. She accepts, but sucks on it instead of biting. She can't think as the Arab up her cunt fucks her more determinedly than she can ever remember being fucked. It's not the length of his cock either. It's the way he's fucking her. Armin fucks her in a manner that suggests that unless she tells him to stop, he could fuck her consistently like this forever. Her pussy is wet, too wet almost as he continues to pound it. His cock slips in and out, in and out, and she thinks that maybe it's too moist. This doesn't seem to worry him though and he just keeps at it, relentless.

Her flow soon stops, and soon he has used his cock to massage the same liquid right back into the walls for her cunt. Her drier pussy is more sensitive and the full magnitude of what is happening to her registers. She starts to scream. There's no restraining it. She has never had as steady a build up to orgasm. She has never had an orgasm that lasted eight minutes. For the eight minutes that it takes for her favorite tracks on the CD player to end Armin's cock proceeds in and out of her until she hangs limply off the side of him, connected to him by his still rock hard dick. He pulls out of her, lets her fall on her back and shoots his load all over her stomach.

The day of the full dress rehearsal comes too soon. Beth hasn't had the strength to see Armin after he quite frankly fucked the living daylights out of her. Her pussy is still tender against her cotton stockings, and she can't imagine that she will be able to put on the rest of the costume. He peeps into her dressing room with a cheeky look in his dark

Middle-Eastern eyes. She smiles coyly as he takes a picture. After encouraging her to just get on with it while he takes pictures in the shadows, she tries to forget that he's here. It's impossible....

Armin notices that she struggles around her pussy and comes closer to examine her. She lets him play doctor, finding her predicament rather amusing, that a woman of her age and physical strength could come so undone at the hands of a penis. But here she was, bruised by cock, and having to go out on stage in twenty minutes and throw her legs open above her head as though all were well between them. He runs his fingers over the stockings covering her pussy and she mouths ouch.

"It can't be that bad little Beth?" he says.

"It is!" she retorts.

He locks the door to the dressing room and quickly pulls the stockings down to her knees. He's on the floor this time and ignores the look of horror on her face. The traffic starts to increase outside in the hall as everyone starts to make their way to the stage to warm up. Beth watches the feet under her dressing room door. Shadows come and go, some linger. She waits for a knock but nothing. She doesn't expect the gentleness of the kisses on her pussy as someone tries the door a few times and then moves on.

Gently Armin places the softest kisses over her pussy. Her clit is still deep pink from his assault, but he knows just how to placate it. He lets his tongue touch the flesh, no more than a touch. Then he kisses the clit again, and then the rest of her vagina. He gives her cunt the most delicate spray of kisses, whispers dancing where a day earlier his dick had stomped. She feels like she might fall over but knows that he won't let her. She braces herself on the table behind her and catches her perfectly made up face in the mirror. She also catches the head between her legs.

Armin circles her clit as softly as he might a wafer, or a marshmallow. He lets her indicate whether or not he can go further, and when her legs lift up and outwards as she places herself on the counter, he lets his tongue make a tentative entry into her pussy. He doesn't go for complete violation, just teasing her entrance, hovering playfully around the hole that he'd bruised unintentionally. She has almost completely forgotten his assault.

The stage manager knocks on her door and urges her to hurry up. She can't respond, as she knows that the sounds that would escape her mouth would be a dead giveaway. Armin starts to lose the control he'd had until now as Beth starts to ooze. Something about her moist cunt-syrup has an animal effect on him. He becomes a monster as his tongue now digs past the entrance and up along the walls of her vagina. The delicate pecks are now a full French kiss. It is with this deep kissing that he finally releases Beth from the tensions of her sensitive pussy. She is reinvigorated as he helps her into her costume and lets her exit the dressing room first.

Beth gives a spirited performance, as does the rest of the ensemble. Armin is satisfied with the shots he gets and has for the first time a real appreciation for this career that he had often mocked. It is only once you see dancers at work that you appreciate what it takes for them to get to that point, on stage, when the audience gets to enjoy the fruits of their labors.

He leaves them to their celebrations and makes his way home, wondering how he might get one more taste of delicious Beth before his flight tomorrow night. Part of him wants to go back and steal her away now, but that would be silly. She has a whole life that has nothing to do with him and tonight is about that life. Besides though, there would be little point in trying to fuck her now, her cunt still needing a few more hours to recover sufficiently.

The light in the loft is soft enough for him to fall asleep without turning it off. His cock has dripped into his pants, probably during his muff-repair efforts in the dressing room. He decides not to attend to it despite the slight discomfort and is soon fast asleep with wild imaginings of what might make for a mind-blowing bon voyage fuck with beautiful Biting Beth.

There is no reason for Armin to go to the dance studio. Besides, it's Sunday, and there would probably be nobody there after last night. Even dancers needed a day off. The only way for him to see her again would be to go over to her apartment. Why had they not exchanged numbers? He decides to make the decision after he's showered. There is always a renewed clarity once one is rid of some of the semen and sexual tension that has built up overnight.

His dick is almost painful when he starts to stroke it. It's been erect for almost three hours as he's tossed in bed contemplating Beth. He goes easy on himself and doesn't give his powerful dick its usual hard-handed lashing. Instead, he gently strokes it from base to tip and back to base in slow steady strokes, light pressure. He loses his erection a few times due to this unusual technique, but eventually, the rhythm registers and his dick plays along. He cums abundantly on the side of the glass paneled shower, pointing the showerhead in this direction to rid the glass of his semen.

It's over coffee that he decides Beth's pussy is worth the embarrassment of being told to fuck off should she not be up to his particular brand of fucking. He throws on a coat and searches briefly of a condom. Finding one, he pockets his wallet and makes for the door. Beth has obviously had the same idea since upon opening the door he finds her standing in his hallway poised to knock. A smile is shared, and she knocks on the open door just for effect.

Inside, she reveals the contents of her bag: two items that would benefit them both, albeit differently. Actually, both items are for her benefit and Armin just gets to fuck her by default. Beth takes the handcuffs first and cuffs Armin to the steel stool at his desk. She uses his scarf to tie his legs to the chairs own. Naked and bound, Armin watches her make use of the other item. It's a cream that decreases the sensitivity of the vagina. She makes careful application in front of him, doing it in such a way that she turns him on. His slithering serpent dances on his lap.

Beth needs to buy enough time for the cream to take effect, and so she goes straight for the kill. He has no way of stopping her teeth from biting into his scrotum. She has an addiction for balls. He's gathered this too late. She knows that he is going to leave her damaged, and so she takes advantage of the opportunity to do some damage of her own first. She doesn't even let him warm up, sinking her teeth immediately into his nuts, then biting into the skin, then his nuts again. His response is somewhere between a laugh and a scream.

She licks his dick, having to use both her hands to hold it. Her tongue is hot on the shaft and then the head before her mouth covers as much of it as possible. He wants to thrust but realizes that he might fall over if he moves around too suddenly. He lets her get on with her agenda, not an altogether unpleasant experience. Her teeth start to tease his cock inside her mouth. He braces himself but is grateful when the entire tool is freed from her mouth without even so much as a nibble. His euphoria is short-lived.

Beth grips with one hand near the tip of his penis and then bites it on the sides all the way up to where her hand is, and then back down. Again a giggle, and a few screams. She really enjoys his responses and gives him a few more bites for good measure. Her mouth wraps over the head of the dick again, above her hand and she frees her grip as she slides down the cock again. Up and down, no teeth this time as she forces the cock straight with her mouth. Satisfied with the completeness of the resultant erection, Beth stands over the cock.

She gets up onto his thighs, a move that surprises him. One foot on either thigh, he thinks she might be offering his mouth her cunt. But then, she squats, reaches back and takes his cock in hand, guiding it inside her. In her squat, she takes four inches inside her, the rest of the dick primed. She kisses him full on his lips as she gets onto her knees, another surprise move as this feeds more of his cock to her pussy. She hugs his neck and goes for his nipples, biting hard as his cock quickly finds the rear of her cunt. Satisfied with her achievement, she proceeds with the rest of her plan.

In the position that she's in, she can move up and down and even back and forth on the cock inside her. Her knees offering her all the support she needs. She can raise herself to bite on his neck, and even nibble on his ears. She can kiss him full on the mouth or even take bites out of his side. She can do all this without releasing the cock inside her. The table behind the chair they're on offering additional support. She bites into his flesh and thanks him for each bite by squeezing the muscles of her cunt around his dick and letting it run a little deeper inside her.

Her cunt is on the verge of an explosion, and she knows that there is no way that she can continue this game after she's cum, not with the ability she's seen his dick to have. She reaches behind him and releases the catch on the cuffs just as she lifts completely off Armin's cock. He quickly loosens the restraints on his legs and charges for her just as she gets on the bed. His cock is inside her before she's on her back.

He manages enough control not to thrust into her completely and knows that in the missionary position it would be very uncomfortable for her. Instead, he places his hands by her side, lower than he would if she were taller. Ten inches fill her at maximum thrust, and this is sufficient for both of them. He takes her over the edge with less than a dozen strokes. Unfortunately, for her cunt, it takes him ten times to finally cum. By the time he shoots his load, Beth knows that her cunt won't be happy with her come morning. Armin has proven himself to be a little more than she can chew....

6 THE VIKING AND THE HONEY BEE

Preface

The last thing the sultry Indian scientist expected was that she would be trapped at a research station in a Nordic snowstorm with a Viking...

Priya took her time in the shower. Her bunker was practically buried under the snow and were it not for the large amber orb revolving a few meters from the roof outside, perched on a metal rod, she would in all likelihood have been lost under the snow forever. But she knew that help was on its way and that it would be here in about five days. She had a month's supply of food left and could relax under the hot water and warm herself up from the inside.

There is something about being stuck out in the middle of nowhere that encourages one to explore oneself. Not only do you find yourself in the philosophical sense, but as Priya had learned, you get to know yourself intimately. And what Priya had learned about her sexy Indian self was that she really loved the feeling of being fucked by a man. This was confirmed for her by the very obvious absence of such a man-person. You see, while she was ever the fashionable feminist, and had purchased a rather interesting collection of vibrators and dildos to help her through her six-month stint in the middle of nowhere, there was no substation for a vibrant robust human-person with a dick attached to its front.

It is one of her purchases, a device called the "ladybug" that was currently occupying her cute little cunt. The vibrator had a multiple array of functions, all able to address various aspects of the female sexual experience at once. With all the time in the world, Priya was indulging in the complete array of excitements. She wished she had more hands, though, the completeness of her self-indulgence sending her off balance.

There is a thick cock-shaped rubber stick that she has already inserted all the way up her cunt. With this entire length inside her, the base of the tool shaped like a ladybug with long tentacles that whiz around in circles, does just that! It whizzes around tickling her dark clit. There is an almost hook-like handle, which ends in a smooth-tipped cock, which can be conveniently inserted into the anus. Under the device is a waterproof control, a panel of buttons that can be pressed with any hand that isn't holding you up. Priya is in no rush and has the tool set to moderate, a setting that should give her an hour or so before she climaxes.

The delicious assault on her pussy especially sends the scientist in her into a lull. She is lost in dreams of every lover she's ever had. She imagines them here now, touching her, wanting her, every one of them inside of her. She allows herself to believe their lips are on hers, on her breasts, and even on parts of her currently occupied by the ladybug. This indulgence is what has made the time she's already spent studying the patterns in the sky over Iceland bearable. It's the nifty little contraptions like the one inside her that make her able to see things through semi-sane.

Her climax is satisfying but predictable. It doesn't matter though, her cunt isn't complaining. She finishes under the water and gets out of the tiny cubicle. After carrying out the necessary admin on the tool and packing it away, she turns the heat up in the main bedroom area of the bunker a little more and sets about moisturizing herself. She treats her pussy to a mini-assault from her own fingers, an exercise that has her reaching for wet wipes to dab her pussy dry. She loves taking her time over every part of her tan skin, richly moisturizing it. She blow-dries her hair naked, half-dancing to the sounds of Maroon 5 on the CD player.

She checks the radio, still naked, and then sits on the seat that she usually occupies when she communicates with the main office. She looks at the tiny red button on the radio and, having convinced herself that nobody is listening to her or trying to get some communication going, she spreads her legs over the seat and lets the leather covering brush her pussy ever so slightly. This foreign touch on this unusual place, a place she's never sat on naked, is enough to send her clit into bloom. She uses the tip of her finger to stop the entrance of her cunt, almost as though she expects a sudden flood to gush forth.

The finger is soon inside her. She rests her head on her arm, which is already resting on the table, and she eyes her middle finger slipping in and out of her cunt. Her cunt tightens at the thought of her rescuers suddenly bursting through the doors and finding her as compromised as she was. The tight cunt around her finger seems to challenge her. She enjoys being challenged and pushes the finger as deep as it will go. Then she slides the index finger inside herself alongside it. The pleasure shoots across the surface of the seat and settles in ripples across her butt. She wiggles around in the chair to adjust to the tingle. Her thighs become a vibrating pleasure center as well as she continues the double-digit dig into her vagina.

Closing her eyes now, she raises her feet onto the metal ring framing the chair that seems suspended in mid-air half a foot of the floor. She tramps down hard on this ring and squeezes the chair between her thighs. Her pussy is flowing again and the liquid trailing out of her settles in a tiny puddle on the seat. She tightens her thigh-grip on the seat as her ass starts to slide around on it. Her fingers make progressively increasing rapid movements, as a third orgasm seems eminent.

Deeper and deeper into herself she goes, tempted for a third finger but not wanting to upset the rhythm. Her pelvis gyrates in the seat as she fucks her fingers, which are absolutely fucking her at the same time. The steady buildup to blast off looms, and then suddenly consumes her entirely. She bangs on the table as for the third time in one morning she manages to bring herself to climax. This final orgasm though strayed ever so slightly off the beaten track and so it ranked up there as the best one yet. Again, the wet-wipes come in handy.

She ignores the thud thud sound coming from the door, then the wall. She cannot believe that the call she had placed for help just this morning was already responded to, despite briefly entertaining this impossibility during her fingering. It would be at least five days before help arrived. And there was no way that there could be anyone out in a storm like this, not even by accident, not near her location. It was five days to the nearest settlement, fragments of a village made modern by electricity and a phone line or two. But the thudding is persistent.

It is only after she has dressed herself sufficiently for inside that she throws a questioning eye at the door. She listens for a cry, a voice, but of course the wind outside would carry any sound away before it even escaped your lips. She allows herself briefly to assume that there actually was someone outside and throws her heavy coat on, her boots too. She makes her way to the door only after she has reported to control that she was going to be checking out a sound outside. She's warned not to, but then again, what if it is someone stuck in the storm like her?

Priya manages to get the door open just a fraction, the snow outside making the task almost impossible. Instantly the door is yanked open by large red gloves, snow filling the doorway, then a backpack. Shortly thereafter, the red gloves reveal themselves to be attached to a Yeti. But of course, Big Foot wouldn't wear clothing so this must be a person. The Viking quickly closes himself inside, gives Priya a piercing blue "thank god" gaze and then tumbles in an icy heap to the floor.

It takes four cups of cocoa to warm Sven up enough for him to be able to introduce himself. He explains his predicament in one sentence, "he's an adventure sportsman who lucked upon the light glowing above her bunker and made his way to it." Grateful that there was life inside and that he could warm up, Sven offers his stash of energy bars, instant soups, and a few slabs of a Belgian brand of chocolates to the survival stocks. This is unnecessary of course but the chocolate does happen to be a favorite of Priya's.

He needs help getting out of his clothing. Priya tries not to look at him but he doesn't seem to care, letting her undress him down to his ice-cold thermal underwear. He stands awaiting instructions and she points him in the direction of the bathroom. She follows him in, setting the water temperature such that while it will warm him up, though it won't do so too quickly. She makes sure he understands the controls and then leaves him to it.

Sven takes two hours in the shower. Fortunately, Priya had prioritized her power usage, sending most of it to the geyser and heating. She really didn't need much light. He comes out of the small bathroom wrapped in a towel, a sight that throws the usually composed scientist. The last thing she could have anticipated was that there would be a large man with white hair, blue eyes, and a broad hairy chest standing in her bunker today. She watches as he takes out a clean pair of long johns and warms them against the heating unit before disappearing into the bathroom to get changed again.

In his absence, Priya is left imagining what he looks like under the towel. She wonders what he tastes like now that he's all cleaned up. Her thoughts quickly fill with constructed images based on the information recently fed to her eyes and she begins to design in her mind a suitable penis for the body that was recently wrapped in her towel and standing in front of her warming his underwear.

The thing about having a big dick and wearing the unflattering all-covering underwear is that every movement gives away the exact location of your cock. And unfortunately for Priya there is no way for her eyes to miss the meat in front of her as Sven makes them both some soup and settles into a long conversation with her about himself. They're both soon in their pajamas under their own blankets caught up in conversations of things more general. Priya finds that she is easily lost in the eyes of the man whose cock had made quite a spectacle of itself earlier. She's also quite impressed with herself because from the outline she gathers that she had got it almost perfect.

The practicality of spooning under all the blankets is a suggestion that was made by Priya for reasons obvious to both her pussy and herself. Sven would never have had the balls to make such a suggestion for fear of being evicted to soon from the safe cocoon, but with his crotch cushioned by Priya's ass his body does just what he hoped would happen only once he had fallen asleep. Sven quite quickly grows a mother of an erection. It happens too quickly for him to move away from Priya, who he hopes to be sleeping. She isn't...

At the risk of looking like a very bad girl, Priya pretends to be in dreamland. She snuggles deeper into Sven's crotch, sending warmth into him that makes his dick even bigger. She moves her ass around in a mock stretch mock adjustment and then is still again, smiling inside as she imagines what must be going through his mind. Occasionally she feels the deliberate rubbing of cock between her cheeks, not too roughly so as not to wake her. Then he is still, a cue for her to "stretch" again.

The moisture between her legs warms her inner thigh. She wants him inside her but she knows she mustn't, not just yet. She has proven that he is open to the possibility and for now, that is enough. She then does the absolutely unthinkable and turns abruptly to face him, freeing his throbbing cock from its warm love-bun. She sinks her head into his chest so as not to give away that she is awake, curls up in the fetal position and then wills herself to sleep knowing that her bedfellow must be cursing her in his head for ending the almost-fuck so soon. It takes everything inside of her not to reach for his dick and guide it up her cunt.

The silence is suddenly thicker than the

dick only inches from her. Her breathing is measured as she falls asleep, much to the frustration of her guest. Sven listens for any sign that she might be awake. She gives him nothing. He tries to sleep but nothing. He stretches around a few times in the hope of waking her. She simply stretches herself back into the fetal position and then finds her spot in his chest. He wants to shake her awake but restrains himself. He wants to part her legs and ram his dick inside her so that by the time she wakes up it's too late for anything but fucking pleasure.

He catches her face in the almost red almost blue light in the room. Immediately he scraps the idea of ramming her with his Nordic log. Something about her face suddenly makes this inappropriate. One thing is certain though, no matter how he does it, he wants to be inside of her. Maybe not as brutishly as he might like, but definitely his cock needs to make the very intimate acquaintance of her pussy. He stares at her in the make-love-to-me-light for what seems like forever.

Too much for him Sven slithers out of bed after convincing himself that Priya is deep in sleep. He more accepted that she was as opposed to convince himself. He makes his way to the bathroom, closes the door behind himself and drops his garb to the floor. The bathroom is colder than the room he's just come from and he tries not to make this realization audibly. There is no time to entertain the thought of a luxurious lathering on his cock for fear of his meat giving in to the cold. A little of his own saliva is sufficient for his hand to get a comfortable hold and provide comfortable enough traction over the large dick to bring himself to a rather quick climax. He pulls the chain as his load escapes the head of his dick and settles on his hand.

Surprised by how little his thoughts were of Priya for the minute or so he beat his meat he decides to go again. He wets his fingers in his mouth and rubs them in circles around the head of his penis, imagining Priya's tongue licking the exposed meat. He slides his fingers down his shaft and then up again in a more solid grip, imagining his cock filling her tiny mouth. He strokes his cock slowly since rapid movements over the semi-stiff shaft give away the task he's taken in hand. Wanking a flaccid cock has a very distinct sound.

Up and down his shaft go his fingers, then his hands, alternately. Suddenly he has no need to cum quickly. He wants a quality orgasm. The fantasies of Priya running through his head seem too good to waist on a quick squirt. His looks at the ceiling as he brings himself closer and closer and then eventually looks back down at his cock as he ejaculates a thick cream that lands on the floor before he can direct it anywhere else. Again, the flushing toilet hides his guilt and eases the awkwardness gnawing at his conscience.

Back in bed it isn't long before he is warm enough to sleep, but not before he has taken the time to really give the exotic honey bee in front of him the once over again. Priya is a tiny package of a woman, beautiful black hair framing her regal Indian face. She is the color of wild honey at sunset. Her tiny hands pillowing her face have the most delicate ten fingers attached to them. She really is every bit the type of woman who makes a man just want to make love to her. She makes fucking seem a vulgar practice reserved for prostitutes.

Sven thinks of what he must look like. Totally unkempt, he's just spent two months trekking across the snow. He's been roughing it in mountains and deserts before that and the journeys show. But he knows that he cleans up nicely, and that he isn't the ugliest boy in the bunch, but he is a tower. He wanders what the likelihood might be of him actually getting to dip his Nordic self into the tiny honey pot. He has known women to enjoy his size, but this woman, this intelligent independent, tiny woman might prefer a gentleman. Not that he couldn't be a gentleman for her, mind you, but if appearances were anything to go by...

He convinces himself that a scientist would be too intelligent to judge a book by its cover. Besides, she's seen his dick, albeit the outline and she has felt it against her. Although the feeling part is a bit sketchy since she could have been sleeping. She must have been sleeping. If not, breakfast might be awkward. Eventually sleep takes him from his erotic fantasy and he allows himself to dream of the possibility of Priya's pussy.

Breakfast is hot chocolate and toast. The protein bars Sven gave make up for the missing fruit, eggs, and bacon. That Priya doesn't feel up to indulging her need for a solid fatty breakfast is expected since the situation inside her one-woman bunker is sufficiently changed for her not to be her normal courteous self. That she doesn't feel sufficiently motivated to feed her guest is something that leaves the almost inappropriately sensitive Sven wondering.

Sven is showered and soon after Priya does too. She has taken it upon herself to clean up before she showers and so once done she waits for him to exit. They have another cup of hot chocolate before she goes into the bathroom to warm herself up and make herself clean all at once.

Priya remembers the stimulation provided her last night. She cleans her pussy gently, irritated slightly that she won't be able to indulge her cunt, but grateful that the possibility of real man pleasure has presented itself. As frustrating as it is, the thought that she might get laid seems to set her entire system at the most remarkable ease. So she lingers ever so briefly over her cunt, checks to see that all her toys are safely out of sight, and gets on with the devastatingly boring task of showering.

The hot water over her turns her nipples into heated mounds that point out in front of her toward forever. The perfection of her breasts often catches even her by surprise and so she cannot help but take the cups of perfection into her hands. She lathers them and pulls ever so gently on her nipples. She massages deep into the sensitive tissue and sends a series of mixed signals to her pussy that soon has the crevice between her thighs weeping.

Priya has started something she can't stop and it isn't long before the same tugging on her nipples is carried out on her clit. She can't afford for Sven to hear her but so what if he does. What judgments could he possibly make after practically burying his cock in her crack last night? In defiance, she quickly shoves a finger inside herself and, moans audible, throwing a look at the bathroom door on the other side of the glass. The moans become silent as sense and reason marry in her mind and she fingers herself with the quiet skill of a convent girl. She's out of the shower in ten minutes.

Sven reads the same page of the book he's taken off the table several times before he closes it. He stares at the lithe beauty curled up on the bed. Priya is also reading. There are no words that come to him immediately that register within as tactful so he swallows all of them. He knows that outside of this bunker there would be no possible chance of the two of them meeting, let alone fucking. But then again, what were the chances that he would stumble on a bunker that wasn't home to six geeks from Ontario with a thesis on the dynamics of the snowflake to complete.

He's never been shy and even thinks of himself as aggressively assertive. But something about this woman, or is it the situation, something about something has him sheepishly pretending to read a book the title of which he hasn't even grasped. Sven continues to steal glances at Priya, who notices this but manages to keep her own staring undiscovered. The fires burning inside both of them threaten to burst out of them, liquid traces of these fires already leaving the places on their persons that they'd like to introduce to each other. Sven's gaze intensifies, his resolve strengthening in his eyes.

"So what would a guy like me have to do to get laid by a girl like you?" Eventually he just goes ahead and asks. He almost dares to hope that the look he sees on Priya's face is relief. It is... He takes the cue from her smile and walks over to her, takes the book from her hands and traces his thick index finger over her lips. Immediately his dick makes a teepee of his underwear. Priya takes the finger into her mouth and arches backward, forcing Sven to sit on the bed if he wants to keep his finger inside her incredibly hot mouth.

The natural rhythm of Sven's decent onto the bed is fluid. He moves as though he anticipated nothing other than the resounding yes that his finger in her mouth signifies. Her movements are as deliberately lingering as she is breathtakingly beautiful. Her own anticipation is such that now that she has confirmed that her vagina will be addressed, she can play with the beast that will be tending her garden, the flower too long cared for by her own hand.

Priya takes the tent in her hands and gently strokes it. Sven straddles her as he enjoys her fingers on his dick. It takes him less than a minute to get out of his long johns, as long to get a complete erection. He kneels over Priya so that his dick hovers over her. She raises herself up, takes it in hand and guides it down into her mouth. Her thermo-sweats are an easy task for Sven who leaves the top on so as not to disturb his dick's escapades in her mouth. He pulls her panties and her pants off in one movement, making a beeline for her pussy.

He soon realizes that he's too tall for his mouth to taste her cunt and so he takes her toes into his mouth. She's never had this done before and writhes at the sensation. He runs a large hand down her leg then up her thigh. His fingers find her cunt and they make the beeline for the entrance. Again, it's his index that proves to be the more active of the appendages. Gentle circles prep the hole and then a slow entrance fills her tight cunt. She immediately wets his hand with an impromptu squirt of her juices. His finger dances inside her in response to the shower.

His finger slides all the way inside her, then all the way out of her. His cock is resting in her mouth as she tilts her head from side to side, sucking on the thick rod at the same time, making him want to thrust, knowing he can't. He wants to savor the body at his disposal. There's no rush. They've got five days at least. Again, his index finger makes a slow entrance into the pussy that has proven to be as perfect as he'd dared to dream. He lets his finger slip out completely again and then bends his head briefly to take a look at the moist cunt sending soft "fuck me" pulses in his direction. He responds with his trusty index.

The fluid inside her pussy warm Priya up rapidly. The thick finger inside her now eases right to the back of her vagina and enjoys heated hugs from every muscle lining the inside of her cunt as it makes its way back out. Sven closes his eyes as he imagines his finger has transformed into his cock and plunges into her again. Her mouth reminds him of the actual location of his penis and so he slowly releases his finger from her depths.

He lifts his dick out of her mouth slowly, her mouth wanting to hold on to it but letting it escape as her cunt receives rushes of warm air from his mouth. As he moves his dick out, he pulls her pussy toward his mouth. He kneels with his legs astride her head, his dick overhead but out of reach. She reaches outward and backward as his mouth lands on her cunt. She pulls her arms back toward herself, through his legs above her own head and then grabs onto his thighs as his tongue finds the inside of her vagina.

His tongue slithers in and out of her pussy with as much power as any prick has ever done. She takes both her hands and wraps them around his dick, milking it as best she can in the position she's in. She must be doing a great job because he starts to grunt and his tongue becomes more insistent on losing itself inside her. His lips cup over her entire cunt, creating a pocket of hot air inside the vacuum while his tongue lines the walls of her cunt with his saliva, extracting her juices simultaneously.

She practically hangs on his penis as Sven begins to thrust, fucking her hands. She tightens her grip in an attempt to give him something to work with. He appreciates her effort and gives her clit the most generous licks, lapping up imagined cream from the delicate indicator of her arousal, now practically bursting. Her vagina weeps for the absence of the tongue but flows as strongly in response to her clit-assault. What's good for one aspect of her sexual anatomy is as good for every other part of her.

His tongue is inside her again and again she milks his cock. The violence of his thrusts now forces the instinctive tightening of her grip again. Again, he fucks her hands. Again, he wishes it was her pussy but his tongue has that covered. She tastes every bit as he's imagined and he assures himself of some dick-dipping but also reminds himself that even getting as far as this hand job and muff was a bonus. So he fucks her delicate hands, grateful just for this.

She doesn't expect the sudden rush of hot semen that covers her stomach but as soon as she realizes he's cumming she tightens her grip on his cock with one final death grip and jerks him off harder until the flow eases. Then she just squeezes while he fucks her hand for her bit more and then nothing. His head comes up only after he has satisfied himself that she has dripped all her own juice into his mouth.

The shower cubicle is a tight squeeze. Warm water washes over Sven and then onto Priya who is technically standing under him. He lathers her up and washes himself off of her. The sticky traces of the fun they've just had run down her and into the swirl that leads from where they stand to somewhere underneath them, and then outside. He lets water run into his mouth, creates his own swirl, runs it around and around then over his teeth and tongue, gargles and then lets this water find the drain as well. She lathers him up but finds that her focus remains on his chest, too distracted by his hands that linger too long over her pussy and then her ass. His hands also find her nipples, cupping her breasts and then fingering the nipples. She starts to milk his dick toward herself as he finally makes his fingers a permanent presence in her pussy.

The thickness of his fingers inside her catches her by surprise even though they've already been to the depths of her cunt. Her vagina struggles against them, not to evict them, but to hold on to them, even though they both know that they have no intention of going anywhere, at least not immediately. She lets her cunt settle around his intruders and allows the completeness of the invasion seep all the way up through her and over her head.

He takes one hand around to her ass and gently positions it so that his middle finger splits her cheeks and its tip touches the entrance to her asshole. The middle finger of the hand in front also divides her pussy, its tip already inside her. He lets the finger at her asshole enter slightly, and then in an almost digging fashion he starts to gently lift her off the ground and then return her to the floor. Each time he lifts her up more of his fingers enter pussy and ass. It's the same every time he puts her down. She keeps losing her own grip on his dick as the fullness of the pleasure she is receiving registers.

She had thought that having more than one of his fingers inside of her was maximum pleasure. To her surprise just one, the middle finger that now bounces her up and down is sufficient to elevate her arousal such that the experience seems strangely complete as is. Somewhere in the back of her mind, she knows that there is more coming. She knows this because the man with her is possessed of the kind of dick that doesn't look like it will take another session of almost fucking. It isn't for nothing that he so meticulously prepares her tight little cunt. His patience is going to need to be rewarded.

The pleasure takes on ever-greater intensities until eventually she holds herself up using his bicep. Both her hands hold on to one arm as his fingers make their way inside her completely. She bites into his arm as he lifts her completely off the ground and toward himself. The tight squeeze makes this a bit of a lengthy process, his fingers digging deeper and deeper every time she gets stuck against the glass. She manages eventually to get her hands around his neck and she pulls herself toward him. He helps her along toward his chest as he removes his fingers from her holes and wraps her legs as far around his waist as possible. They lock behind him.

Each of his hands firmly grips one of her butt cheeks and he positions her so that his penis is sandwiched between her pussy and his stomach. His tip is above his naval and so he makes this the destination for Priya's cunt. Up and down he slides her, rubbing the full length of his tool against her clit. Eventually her vagina connects with his dick-head. His cock is so rock hard that he can move her in circles over his dick and the tool follows the movement for as long as it remains in touch with her pussy. Her cunt starts to salivate at the thought of this new intruder. Her pussy drizzles the liquid that will make penetration possible.

She grabs his neck tighter as she feels the pressure from the dick now wanting to get inside her. He holds her ass tight as he moves slowly from side to side, letting her adjust to each inch as he goes. Four inches, five inches, six inches and she seems to be full. He tries for a few more wriggles but her body has tensed at the thought of the entire rod inside her. He decides to let her get comfortable with what he's already fed her. She stretches her legs further around him to take some more. Not yet, her pussy tells her.

She tries in vain to lift herself up off his

dick slightly, needing to breathe. For reasons of its sheer size, she is somehow convinced that the entire cock is inside her. She tries to move herself around and only once she slips a little lower does she get a better idea of her predicament. Suddenly the most important things to her now are his hands that seem to hold her safely above the remainder of his dick. His hands are the only protection she has from the excessive length of cock that looms threateningly below. Priya suddenly feels like she's caught in one of those games of trust where you close your eyes and let yourself fall without looking behind you, trusting blindly that there will be somebody there to catch you.

Sven doesn't so much thrust as he moves her around on his dick, sensing her innermost thoughts. Priya can but push toward his stomach and then behind herself, rocking backward and forward. The up and down of the movement is in Sven's hands, and while he wants to rest his meat deep inside her and get on with it, the delicate fragility of the beauty around his waist begs a different approach. So he continues to gently move her around on his dick, augmenting his own frustration, his dick begging for a couple of jabs, indulging itself occasionally much to the surprise of both Priya and Sven.

Each time his dick takes on a life of its own and throws four or five stabs inside of her Sven murmurs an apology. She knows enough about the male physique to know that it's largely involuntary and so she silently forgives. Part of her enjoys the rudeness of the violation. Part of her wants it. But the part of her that actually experiences it is not as enthusiastic. Perhaps it's the position she's in, perhaps the location. Maybe she would be more accommodating on her back on a bed, or even straddling him on a bed where she could control the pace of penetration.

Priya isn't a control freak. She likes to let a man do what he's meant to do. In her mind, a man is so perfectly designed to fuck the shit out of any pussy that to want him to do anything else is sinful. She likes being fucked by a man who likes to fuck. Knowing that Sven is holding back has her wandering if he too is having the same problem with the setting as she is. But the hardness of his meat inside her seems to suggest that he has no problem at all.

They both lose time, feeling like they've been in the shower forever. They have, and it doesn't matter. The water doesn't disappoint, staying hot for the entire duration of the fuck session. It takes ninety minutes for Sven to build himself up to climax. The walls of Priya's pussy have already flowed several times with a lot more than water. She's had several exhilarating orgasms before her back finds the shower wall and the gentleman becomes a brut. Unable to contain himself, and also feeling like he deserves a little more of the pussy he's just so completely pleased, Sven thrusts into Priya, a good four more inches. Satisfied with this he begins a rapid series of thrusts that see him cum all over her breasts, having just managed to withdraw and return his dick to the original sandwich position, letting the outside of Priya's pussy do the final grind.

The embrace locks for a moment longer before they get on with the business of cleaning each other up again. Sven enjoys deep kisses while he continues to tease Priya, fingering her every time she tries to leave the cubicle. Eventually she's had eleven orgasms. Knowing that she won't do this incredible lover justice with a mere hand job she manages to work herself into a corner of the cubicle so that she can crouch slightly and take his cock into her mouth. She sucks on it gently, going as far down the shaft of it as she can. He relaxes with his hands holding up the cubicle walls as he watches her brave attempt on his mammoth dick. She manages for another load, this time in her mouth, swallowing it down with a smile.

There is nothing to it now and they

jump into bed, snuggle up, and sleep soundly for a whole night and most of the next day.

The setting could not have been better, a warm toasty love nest in a white dessert in subzero terrain. It screamed "lovemaking" despite the desperation that could have hung in the air. The assurance of rescue however is what ensured that both Sven and Priya slept soundly. With just over two days to go before they're rescued the entire atmosphere in the bunker hangs thick with the anticipation of fucking instead.

Despite the marathon fuck of the night before they both have nothing but sex on the brain. Even their sleep is disturbed by the anxiety that too soon they're going to be disturbed by a group of people trekking across in a storm to come and save them from being buried alive in a snowstorm. It seems such a nuisance that it should take them a measly five days to get here. There's even secret shared hope that the rescuers themselves become lost in the storm, just to buy them a little more fuck time.

The ideas around the actual copulation differ though. But it is safe to say that there is greater anxiety relative to the time left inside the space. It's the possibilities for exploration open to them now that they've passed the awkward "shall we fuck" phase that have them particularly anxious. Would they be able to fit it all in and would either of them object to some of the intimate fantasies either entertained about the other?

Size is a strange thing when it comes to fucking. People seem to be drawn to extremes, despite the best sex being had with people who are comfortable underneath or on top of us. But because the two of them differ so in size, this is the thing that most excites both of them. Priya wants to challenge her pussy and Sven wants to challenge his patience. Priya also wants to know that she has opened up a whole other possible stream of lovers for future reference, always having limited herself to shorter men who, while also sufficiently endowed, never really stretched other parts of her. With Sven, she actually needs to reach. This adds a new dynamic to the process of lovemaking. Also, Sven is curious as to the physical possibilities of a female body, him also having limited himself to the taller of the species on the assumption of deeper and more accommodating cunt.

Priya wants Sven to maybe ease up on the gentlemanly behavior. She actually wants to feel what she knows he could possibly do when he performs full strength. She felt even through the restrictions of the shower cubicle's proportions that he was holding back from full performance. She didn't want him to hold back, but he was just being so nice. It was the deepest desire of her cunt to feel him full-throttle.

Sven on the other hand has his own ideas. He thinks that there is no way that he could possibly expect the beautiful Priya to simply lay back and let him have his Nordic way with her. Everything about her says she should be handled with care. Of course, Priya is nothing like that and in fact has found herself quite bored with chivalry. And therein lays the conundrum.

The size of the erection pressing up against her excites her. Priya hasn't fully awoke yet and Sven is still asleep having jumped back into bed after a bathroom visit that involved brushing his teeth and taking a very long pee. Both their thoughts and desires have managed to create an air of anticipation that hides itself under the covers with the parts of their bodies that should be meeting this anticipation head on. Sven's cock has the right idea. His snores frustrate the horny Priya who slips out of bed, brushes her own teeth and then proceeds to make two very loud cups of hot chocolate.

Sven is already sitting up by the time

she offers him his cup in bed. They sip their cups to half in total silence. Sven is the first to test the waters, running his hand along the side of her leg under the covers. Her legs part as his finger get to her thigh and he makes his way between her legs where his hand is met with a blooming cunt already moist through her clothes. Her cup is immediately put down and she lies on her back, aching to be fucked. Sven fills his mouth with hot chocolate and doesn't swallow for the duration of the time it takes him to remove all Priya's clothes. He then proceeds to settle his hot tongue on her pussy, licking hard along the exterior surface of her cunt before finding his way inside her.

Priya grabs onto his head as she pushes her cunt into his mouth. Sven digs deeper and deeper with his tongue, lapping juices from the far reaches of her cunt. His own cock begins to throb and he realizes that the smell and taste of Priya has sent a signal to his dick that his head cannot override. He removes his clothes, the one-piece long johns that have become his second skin, as best he can without removing his tongue from inside her, lifting his head from her pussy only once he has freed his dick.

Once she feels the head of his dick miss the entrance to her waiting pussy, she hangs onto his neck and lifts herself off the bed so that she wraps her legs around his waist. She actually hangs around his lower back as she attempts to accost his dick herself. The intensity of the entry is unexpected, the swiftness of the thrust throws her and she winces. He realizes that he's probably gone too deep too quickly and he lowers himself so that she has her back and ass on the bed. She stops him as he tries to withdraw out of courtesy. He pauses, giving her the time she needs.

Priya slowly pushes her butt into the bed, releasing some dick. She then pushes her pussy forward then upward, taking it back in. She repeats the motion, releasing less and less dick while swallowing more and more on each thrust. She reaches her max solo effort at around half of Sven's cock, needing him to help now if any more of him is going to get inside her. He withdraws almost completely and the slowly fills her up inch by inch, watching her face closely as he gets an impressive three quarters of his man-pole inside her. She braces herself on his arms again and he withdraws, reinserting the same three quarters.

He does this for a few long thrusts. The three quarters seems to be what she can safely take. Then he tries for more. He doesn't withdraw. Instead, he makes short stabs into her cunt. Each stab tries to insert another millimeter inside her. So millimeter by millimeter he works up to another inch, and then another. There is no withdrawing, just a steady advancing into her. She smiles, breathing deep. She has no intention of letting any discomfort show, needing him to do what he needs to do. There's a brief struggle with the final inch, but then slowly, gently, a little force, a little pressure, and their waists touch. Sven's massive cock has made it all the way.

That it is possible has been proven, but the dick is just a little too much for the comfort of the delicate Priya. So after a few circular thrusts and having satisfied both of them as to the elasticity of cunt, Priya eases some of the meat out of her. She gets back to the three quarters that had them both smiling and that becomes the benchmark. Sven is satisfied with this and readies himself to make the absolute most of Priya's extremely generous cunt, even though he's now a quarter shy of total penetration.

They realize that no more of the rod is needed to really satisfy her. He also doesn't need to get all the way inside her for his dick to be fulfilled. Even now that they know that it's possible, it isn't necessary. He thrusts into her and withdraws almost completely each time, maximizing the impact his cock has on the inside of her cunt. She tries but fails to count his thrusts but Priya is sure that there are hundreds. It feels like hundreds. Hours drift by without change of position. It seems unnecessary when they both seem to be getting maximum pleasure from the mundane missionary.

Priya again wraps her arms around Sven's neck, as he inadvertently inserts what can't be more than another inch into her. His withdrawal is less and less complete and she realizes that there is nothing she can do to stop him now from getting to the end. She accepts that there might be more dick shoved inside her than she can handle, especially without the restriction that was offered by the tiny shower cubicle. That shower had actually protected her from all this cock that now had no barrier, nothing to stop it from completely invading her.

It's her own pussy that betrays her in the end. Her climax is a delicious combination of her internal juices that robs her cunt walls of the traction they had had which kept at least some of Sven's cock at bay. But now as she climaxes and loses herself completely in her orgasm he has nothing to stop his dick from slipping inside her completely. His massive dick does just that. The last couple of thrusts, possibly a dozen, are completely inside her. Were it not for the fucking fantastic orgasm she was having she might have been calling for medical attention, but instead her pussy generously accommodates all of Sven and carries him to as glorious a climax as she's just had.

Neither of them hears the notice that the storm has dissipated. They don't hear the call that there will be no need for a rescue and that all has returned to normal. They fuck several times between meals and sleeps and don't even bother to check the radio. Only on the day of the anticipated rescue does Priya eventually get the message, which has now morphed into a frantic request from her bosses for her to get in touch or they'll have to send the rescue team along to see if she's okay. The sun is shining outside when they walk into the snow. Sven is reluctant to leave but after a solid "one for the road" fuck the adventurer in him makes for the wild white yonder, leaving the satisfied scientist to get on with the business at hand.

AUTHOR'S NOTE

Readers: I want to expand a few of the stories to see where the characters can be explored further. If there are any of the stories that you would like to read more about again, I'd love to hear from you!

Visit my blog at www.kellenprime.com

Join my newsletter for free exclusive previews
http://www.kellenprime.com/in

Follow me on Twitter at
http://www.twitter.com/kellenprime

Like my page on Facebook at
http://www.facebook.com/kellenprime

Discover my books at major ebook retailers everywhere.